If it is profit that a man is after, he should become a merchant, and if he does the job of a bookseller then he should renounce the name of poet. Christ forbid that the business followed by such creatures should furnish a man of spirit with his occupation.

Every year I spend a fortune, and so it would be a fine thing if I followed the example of the gambler who placed a bet of a hundred ducats and then beat his wife for not filling the lamps with the cheapest oil.

So print my letters carefully, on good parchment, and that's the only recompense I want. In this way bit by bit you will be the heir to all my talent may produce.

ARETINO
from a letter dated 22nd June 1537, sent from Venice

CASANOVA

STEFAN ZWEIG

CASANOVA

Translated by
Eden and Cedar Paul

PUSHKIN PRESS
LONDON

To Maxim Gorky

Original text © William Verlag AG Zurich
First published in Great Britain in 1929

This edition first published in 1998 by
Pushkin Press
123 Biddulph Mansions
Elgin Avenue
London W9 1HU

Second impression 2001

British Library Cataloguing in Publication Data:
A catalogue record for this book is available
from the British Library

ISBN 0 1901285 18 9

Set in 10½ on 13½ Baskerville
and printed in Britain
by Sherlock Printing, Bolney, West Sussex
on Legend Laid paper

CONTENTS

Il me dit qu'il est un homme libre,
citoyen du monde.

MURALT, WRITING OF CASANOVA
IN A LETTER TO
ALBRECHT VON HALLER, JUNE 21, 1760

THE MAN AND THE BOOK

He tells himself the story of his life.
This is his entire literary output—but
what a story!

CASANOVA is an exceptional instance, a chance intruder in world literature, above all because this famous charlatan has as little right in the pantheon of creative geniuses as the name of Pontius Pilate has in the Creed. His rank as imaginative writer is as questionable as his invented title of nobility, Chevalier de Seingalt: the few verses he penned hastily between bed and the gaming table in honour of one lady or another reek of musk and academic paste; one who would read his *Icosameron*, a monstrosity of a Utopian romance, needs the patience of a lamb under the hide of a jackass; and when the excellent Giacomo begins to philosophize, it is hard to keep from yawning. In very truth, Casanova has as little claim to enter the company of great writers as he has to a place in the Almanach de Gotha; in both he is a parasite, an unwarrantable intruder.

Nevertheless, this son of a shady actor, this unfrocked priest, this un-uniformed soldier, this notorious cheat (a superintendent of police in Paris describes him in his dossier as a *fameux filou*), is able to ruffle it for a large part of his life among emperors and kings, and dies at last in the arms of a great nobleman, the Prince de Ligne: and, though he seems a mere pretender in the world of letters, one among many, ashes to be blown about by the winds of time, his roaming shade has found a place for itself among the immortals. Here, too, is an even more remarkable fact. Whereas nearly all his noble fellow countrymen, the sublime poets of Arcady, the "divine" Metastasio, the distinguished Parini, and the rest of them, are to be found only on the upper shelves of the libraries, have become material for dry-as-dust studies—his name, uttered with an indulgent smile, is still on everyone's lips. According to all earthly probability, his erotic Iliad will still be very much alive, and will still find admiring readers, long after *La Gerusalemme liberata* and *Il pastor fido* have been gathering the dust of ages upon their unread tops. At one stride, the cunning adventurer has outdistanced all the great writers of Italy since Dante and Boccaccio.

Stranger yet, for such immense winnings, Casanova has staked nothing at all; he has overreached fate, and secured immortality by artifice. This gamester

knows naught of the overwhelming sense of responsibility which burdens the true artist. Not for him the
corvée of unsociability which severs the writer over-
burdened with work from the warm world of everyday life. Casanova knows naught of the dread pleasure with which the author plans a book, or of the
eagerness for perfection which is his tragic associate
and torments like an unquenchable thirst. No part of
his experience is the mute but masterful and ever
unsatisfied demand of fancied shapes to be endowed
with earthly circumstantiality, the longing of ideas to
be liberated from earth and to soar upwards into the
ether. He knows nothing of sleepless nights, followed
by days which must be spent in the dull and slavish
labour of polishing words and phrases, until at
length the meaning shines with all the colours of the
rainbow through the lens of speech; nothing of the
multifarious but unseen toil of the creative writer,
unrewarded and often unrecognized for generations;
nothing of the man of letters' heroic renunciation of
the joys of life. Casanova, as everyone knows, took
life easily enough, sacrificing not a morsel of his joys,
not an hour of his sleep, not a moment of his pleasures, to the stern goddess of immortality. He never
lifted a finger to secure fame; and yet to him, born
under a fortunate star, fame has come superabun-
dantly. As long as he had a gold piece or two in his

pocket, a drop of oil with which to keep the flame of love alight, as long as he was still able to throw the dice, he had no thought of keeping company with the serious-minded spirit of art, or of soiling his fingers with ink. Only when all doors had been closed upon him, when women began to laugh at his amorous advances, when he was lonely, a beggar, and impotent, when the joys of life had become irrecoverable memories—only then, when he was a shabby and splenetic old man, did he turn to work as a substitute for livelier experiences. Only then, urged on by the lack of pleasure, by boredom, tormented by anger as a neglected cur is tormented by the mange, did he grumblingly set to work to tell the story of the septuagenarian Casaneus-Casanova, the story of his own life.

He tells the story of his own life. This is his entire literary output—but what a story. Five novels, twenty comedies, a sheaf of novelettes and episodes, and a superabundance of fascinating situations and anecdotes, trodden like grapes to form the must of an exuberant narrative: the result is a life history which assumes the aspect of a perfectly rounded work of art though it has not had the ordering touch of the master of literary art. Herein we find the most convincing solution of that which at first seems the inexplicable mystery of his fame. What makes Casanova a genius

14

is, not the way in which he tells the story of his life, but the way in which he has lived it. That life itself is this great artist's workshop, is at once his matter and his form. To this work of art, really and truly his own, he has given himself up with the creative ardour which imaginative writers in general devote to verse or to prose, glowing with the fiery resolve to stamp every moment, every still undecided possibility, with the highest dramatic expression. What another has to invent, he has actually experienced; what another must form in imagination, he has figured forth in his warm and voluptuous body; that is why, in this case, the pen and the fancy have no need to adorn the truth; enough that they should take a tracing of an existence which has already been effectively staged. No writer of his day, and scarcely a writer since (unless it be Balzac), has invented so many variations and situations as Casanova experienced; and throughout a whole century no other man has ever lived a life swinging in such bold curves. Compare, as regards pure wealth of happenings (not as regards spiritual substance or depth of experience), the biographies of Goethe, Jean-Jacques Rousseau, and other contemporaries, with Casanova's own. How much they seem, regarded in the light of that comparison, to run in grooves, how monotonous, how narrow, how provincial appear these lives—purposeful though they are, and animated with creative will—beside the elemental career of the adventurer, who changes countries, towns, estates, occupations, worlds, and women, as easily as he changes his shirt; who is everywhere and instantly at home; who is always ready to welcome new surprises. These others are but dilettantes in matters of enjoyment, just as Casanova is a dilettante in the world of letters. That is the eternal tragedy of the man of the spirit, that he, yearn though he may to fulfil his mission by experiencing all the volup-tuousness of life, is nevertheless bound to his task, slave of his workshop, fettered by self-imposed duties, tied to order and to earth. Every true artist lives the larger half of his life alone, engaged in a duel with his creative work. Not in direct experience, but only through the mirror of fancy, may he enjoy the multi-plicity of existence. To none but the uncreative, to none but the man of pleasure, to none but him who lives for life's own sake, is it permitted to give himself unreservedly and directly to reality. One who aims at a goal must renounce the delights of hazard. What the artist creates in imagination is, as a rule, what he is debarred from actually living.

On the other hand the counterparts of these artists, easy-going men of pleasure, usually lack the power of describing their manifold experiences.

They lose themselves in the passing moment, so that when the moment has passed it is lost for ever, whereas the artist knows how to perpetuate the most trifling experience. Thus do the ends gape, instead of rounding the full circle; one lacks the wine, while the other lacks the goblet. Insoluble paradox: men of action and men of pleasure have more experience to report than any creative artist, but they cannot tell their story; the poietes, on the other hand, must fable, for they have seldom had experiences worth reporting. Imaginative writers rarely have a biography, and men who have biographies are only in exceptional instances able to write them.

Casanova is a splendid, almost unique exception. In him at length we find a man afire with the love of pleasure, a man who plucks at the fleeting hour, grasps at the skirts of happy chance, and is endowed by fate with the most extraordinary adventures; a man with an amazingly good memory, and one whose character knows nothing of inhibitions. This man tells us the tremendous story of his life, tells it without any moral restraints, without poetical adornments, without philosophic embroidery; he gives us a plain, matter-of-fact account of his life as it actually was, passionate, hazardous, rascally, reckless, amusing, vulgar, unseemly, impudent, lascivious, but always tense and unexpected. He is

moved to tell his story; not by literary ambition, not
by boastfulness or penitence, or an exhibitionist urge
toward confession; but by a straightforward desire to
tell it. He tells it, therefore, simply and easily; as a
veteran in a tavern, pipe in mouth, talks his best
when he relates a few crisp and perhaps rather sala-
cious adventures to unprejudiced auditors. Here the
narrator is not a fabulist, an inventor, but the master
of poesy of life itself, life whose world is richer than
any world of fancy. All that Casanova need do is sat-
isfy the most modest of the demands made upon the
artist; he must render the almost incredible, credible.
To this task he is fully equal, despite the language of
the memoirs, a somewhat awkward French. Not
even in a dream, however, did this tremulous, gouty,
and discontented old fellow, who passed the evening
of his days in his sinecure occupation of librarian,
ever think that in times to come these memoirs of
his would be regarded by men of letters and histori-
ans as the most valuable record of eighteenth-cen-
tury life. What would he have thought if
Feltkirchner, the steward at Dux, had prophesied
that a hundred and twenty years later there would
be founded in Paris a Casanova Society, simply in
order to scrutinize every fragment of the adventurer's handwriting, to check every date, and to discover if possible the names of the ladies represented

in the book by blanks. Paris was forbidden ground; Feltkirchner, his housemate, was his enemy; and the good Giacomo, vain though he was, would have regarded such a prophecy as an ill-natured jest.

In truth we can congratulate ourselves that, despite his vanity, Casanova had no inkling that he was destined to become famous, and therefore was never inclined to pull out the moral, the pathetical, or the psychological stop—for only one who is free from purposes of this order can preserve the heedless and therefore elemental straightforwardness characteristic of the memoirs. The old gamester sits down to his writing table at Dux with his usual composure, and the writing of his book is his last win at the gaming table. But he never learns that he is a winner, for he departs this life before the cards are turned. Yet he has won immortality, nonetheless. Nothing will ever dislodge him from his place among the immortals, this sometime librarian at Dux, from his place beside his adversary Monsieur de Voltaire and other famous authors. We have not yet finished writing the story of his life, and its inexhaustible treasures are continually attracting fresh literary craftsmen to pen works of fancy about him. Unquestionably he has been a winner in the game of life, this *commediante in fortuna*, this man who was ever ready to try his luck; and no protests of posterity will deprive him of his gains. Some may despise him for his immorality, others may convict him of errors of historical fact, and yet others may disavow him as an artist. But there is one thing that no objector can do—make an end of him! For since he lived his life and wrote his story, no romancer and no thinker has invented a more romantic tale than that of his life, or fabled a stranger personality than Casanova's.

LIKENESS OF CASANOVA
IN YOUTH

*Do you know that you are an
exceedingly handsome man?*

SAID BY FREDERICK THE GREAT
TO CASANOVA, WALKING IN THE
PARK AT SANS-SOUCI (1764)

IN THE THEATRE of a petty capital, the singer has
just finished her aria with a fine coloratura passage; there has been a thunder of applause; but now,
during the recitative, the attention of the audience
has wandered. The fops are paying visits to the
boxes; the ladies are eyeing people through their
lorgnons, and are daintily eating jelly or sipping
orange-tinted sherbet, paying scant attention to the
antics of Harlequin and Columbine on the stage.
Suddenly all eyes are turned inquisitively towards a
stranger who, with the easy air of a man of distinction, makes a late entry into the auditorium. Of
Herculean figure, he is attired as a man of wealth.
An upper garment of ash-tinted velvet falls in rich
folds over an embroidered brocade waistcoat and

21

expensive lace; the darker lines of his vesture are relieved by the gleam of gold lace, which extends from the clasp at his neck on either side of his shirt-frill down to the top of his silk stockings. In his right hand, negligently held, is a white-plumed hat. An aroma of the latest fashionable scent radiates from the unknown, as he leans in an elegant posture against the balustrade, his left hand, gleaming with rings, resting on the jewelled hilt of his sword. As if unaware that he is the cynosure of all eyes, he lifts his golden *lorgnon*, and with feigned indifference scans the boxes. There is a rustle of whispered inquiries. Who is it? A prince? A rich foreigner? The whisperers draw one another's attention to the diamond-spangled order which hangs from the scarlet ribbon that crosses his breast, the order he has disguised with so many brilliants that no one recognizes it for one of the papal spurred crosses which are as common as blackberries. The singers on the stage are quick to note the distraction of the audience, and their efforts are relaxed. The ballet dancers, peeping from the wings across the violins and the cellos, wonder whether this stranger is a person whose acquaintance is worth making.

Before anyone has been able to solve the riddle of the newcomer's identity, or to learn whence he has come, the ladies in the boxes have been quick to note how handsome he is, how fine a figure of a man. He is tall and broadshouldered, his hands are strong and sinewy, his frame is tense as steel without a line of softness in it. He stands lightly poised, his head a little lowered, like that of a bull before the charge. Seen in profile, his face recalls those seen on Roman coins, so finely chiselled is it in every line. The forehead is splendidly arched beneath the chestnut hair; the nose is aquiline, the chin powerful, and beneath the chin is a big Adam's apple (which women regard as a sure sign of virility). His features, one and all, give unmistakable proof of dash, resolution, a conqueror's gifts. Only the lips are soft, being red and sensual, gently curved, while peeping from between them, like the flesh of a pomegranate, gleam the white teeth. As the handsome stranger scans the audience, though he does it in leisurely fashion, we note a certain impatience in the eyes that flash from beneath the arched bushy brows. He has a hunter's glance, the expression of one surveying a quarry, of one who is ready to pounce upon his prey. As yet, however, he is not fully aflame, while his eyes roam along the boxes, and while, paying scant heed to the men, he samples (as a merchant samples wares) the women whose bare necks and shoulders are visible in the shadowy nests. He looks at them one after another, fastidiously, with the eye of a connoisseur, knowing that they are contemplating him in return. As he does so, his sensual lips part a little more widely, and a smile begins to form, a smile that almost reminds us of the snarl of a beast ready to bite. As yet this smile is not directed towards any one woman in particular; it is for them all, for women in general, the essential woman whose warm nudities are hidden under their clothes. Now, in one of the boxes, he recognizes an acquaintance. Instantly his gaze is arrested, his eyes, which a moment before were impudently questioning, show a velvety glitter; he draws his left hand away from his sword hilt, while in his right he grips his heavy plumed hat more firmly; and he moves to greet his lady friend, a word of recognition on his lips. Gracefully he bends to kiss her proffered fingers, and speak to her courteously. For her part, the lady is confused, his caressive tone disturbs her, but she manages to control herself and introduces the stranger to her companions saying: "Le Chevalier de Seingalt."

There are the usual polite formalities. The guest is invited to a place in the box. A conversation ensues. By degrees Casanova raises his voice a little, till it dominates the others. Like a trained actor, he articulates clearly, and tends more and more to speak to a wider audience than that of the box he has entered.

He wants all those nearby to hear what excellent
French and Italian he speaks, and how cleverly he
can quote Horace. As if by chance, he has let one of
his hands fall upon the breastwork of the box in such
a way as to display the lace ruffle on his sleeve, and
to show the sparkle of the great solitaire on his finger.
Then, taking from his pocket a diamond-studded
snuffbox, he offers the gentlemen some Mexican
snuff, saying: "My friend the Spanish ambassador
sent it to me yesterday by special courier." When
one of the gentlemen admires the miniature painted
on the snuffbox, he says indifferently, but loud
enough to be heard through the auditorium: "A present from my friend and gracious lord the Elector of
Cologne." Though he seems to say these things quite
casually, the braggart is all the while eyeing those to
right and left of him with the questing gaze of a bird
of prey, that he may judge the effect of his words.

He sees that he is the centre of all eyes; he feels
that the women are eager to know more about him;
and he grows bolder. With an adroit turn of the conversation, he is able to make it lap over into the
adjoining box, where the prince's inamorata is listen-
ing well-pleased (he is sure of it) to his admirable
Parisian French. Preening himself before this handsome woman, he utters a gallantry, which she smil-
ingly answers. Now his acquaintance has no choice

but to introduce the Chevalier to this exalted dame.
He has gained his end. Next day at noon he will dine
in distinguished company; tomorrow evening, in one
of the palaces of the nobility, he will propose a little
game of faro, and will plunder his host; tomorrow
night he will sleep with one of these pretty women,
whose nudity he has already relished in his mind.
He will succeed in doing all these things thanks to
his bold, self-confident, and energetic entry, his conqueror's will, and the virile beauty of his dark-
skinned face. To these he owes everything: the smiles
of women, the solitaire on his finger, the diamond
watchchain and the gold lace, credit at the bank, the
friendship of men of title, and, best of all, freedom to
roam at will through an infinitely varied life.

Meanwhile the prima donna has begun a new
aria. Bowing profoundly, acknowledging urgent invi-
tations from gentlemen charmed by his conversation,
and graciously invited to her *levee* by the prince's
inamorata, Casanova takes his leave and returns to
his place. There he sits down, his left hand again
poised on the hilt of his sword, while he leans forward to listen to the song. Behind him runs a whisper from box to box, a buzz of questions, which are
all answered: "The Chevalier de Seingalt." Nothing
more is known of him. No one can say whence he
has come, or why, or whither he is going. But the

name ripples through the eager auditorium, and at length makes its way across the footlights to the stage, where the singers have been no less curious as to his identity. On hearing it, a little Venetian dancer laughs contemptuously, and exclaims: "Chevalier de Seingalt? The swindler! He is Casanova, the son of *La Buranella* he is the *abate* who seduced my sister five years ago; old Bragadin's court jester; the braggart, the rascal, the adventurer." Nevertheless, this cheerful young lady does not seem to take his misdeeds altogether unkindly, for she nods to him from the wings, and kisses her hand to him coquettishly. Catching sight of this, he remembers who she is, and is quite unperturbed. He is sure that she will not try to put a spoke in his wheel, will not interfere with his plucking of the distinguished geese. No doubt she will be ready enough to sleep with him tonight.

THE ADVENTURERS

Does she know that your whole fortune
is the stupidity of your fellowmen?
CASANOVA TO CROCE,
THE CARD-SHARPER

F ROM THE CLOSE of the Seven Years' War down
to the outbreak of the French Revolution, calm
prevailed throughout Europe for a quarter of a century. The great dynasties of Habsburg, Bourbon,
and Hohenzollern had fought till they were tired.
The burghers sat at home smoking their pipes in
comfort; the soldiers powdered their pigtails and pol-
ished the muskets for which they no longer had any
use; the countries, so long tormented, could at length
enjoy a quiet doze. But the rulers found life tedious
without any wars. They were bored to death, all the
German and Italian and other petty princes, in their
diminutive capitals; and they looked round eagerly
in search of amusement. Infinitely tedious did they
find it, these little grandees, these electors and dukes,
in their newly built and damp *rococo* palaces. It was
dull for them there, despite all their pleasure gardens

29

and fountains and orangeries, despite their dungeons and galleries and game-parks and treasure chambers.

With the aid of money extorted from their subjects, and with manners learned from Parisian dancing masters, they ape Trianon and Versailles, each one of them fancying himself cast for the part of *le roi soleil*. Ennui even leads them to become patrons of the arts, to affect literary tastes, so that they correspond with Voltaire and Diderot; collect china, coins, old masters; have French comedies and Italian operas staged at their court theatres, showering their favours on foreign artists—for only one of them, the ruler in Weimar, has had the good sense to invite to his court a few Germans, Schiller, Goethe, and Herder by name. Their only other amusements are boar-hunts and water pageants. As always when people of the fashionable world find life tedious, theatricals and dancing assume peculiar importance. That is why these princes outbid one another, that is why they set diplomacy at work, in order to secure the most lively entertainers, the best dancers, instrumentalists, castrati, philosophers, alchemists, and organists. Gluck and Handel, Metastasio and Hasse, are lured from one court to another, turn by turn with cabalists and cocottes, firework artists and huntsmen, illuminators and ballet masters. Each one of these petty princes wants his palace to be distinguished by the presence of the newest, the most splendid, the most fashionable among the famous, being moved rather by the desire to outdo his brother prince at the court twenty miles away than by any reasonable motive. At one court after another they have secured efficient masters of ceremonies, have built fine theatres and opera houses, and have graced these with successful performances; only one thing more is needed to relieve the monotony of life, and to make the eternal round of social intercourse among fifty or sixty titled families assume the aspect of really distinguished society —notable visitors, interesting guests, cosmopolitan strangers, a few raisins for the dough of provincial boredom, a breath from the great world to clear the stuffy atmosphere of a capital containing no more than thirty streets.

They hear of a court, and in a trice they flock thither, the adventurers, in hundreds of masks and disguises. No one can tell you whence they come. They arrive in travelling carriages, or maybe in coaches of the best English pattern, to rent the finest front rooms in the most expensive inns. They wear brilliant uniforms, said to be those of some Indian or Mongolian army; and they bear pompous names, false as the jewels they flaunt on their shoebuckles. They speak all languages; claim to be the familiar friends of rulers and other people of importance;

have served in every army of note; and have studied at all the universities. Their pockets bulge with memoranda of schemes; their mouths are full of promises; they plan lotteries, new taxes, alliances, factories; they offer women and orders and castrati. Although they have not as much as half a dozen gold pieces in their purses, they whisper in every ear that they know the secret of the philosopher's stone. They devise a new trick for each court. In one they let it be given out that they are freemasons and Rosicrucians; in another, where the ruler has a lust for money, they claim to be extraordinarily well versed in the law of transmutation and in the writings of Theophrastus. To a prince whose chief interest is in the fair sex, they offer their services as pimps; to one who has warlike ambitions, they present themselves as spies; to a ruler with a taste for literature and the arts, they introduce themselves as philosophers and poetasters. They snare the superstitious with horoscopes; the credulous with schemes for enrichment; the gamblers with false cards; and the unsuspicious with a veneer of good breeding. But whatever the role they choose, they are careful to invest it with an aroma of mystery which will make it more interesting than ever. Like will-o'-the-wisps, flaring of a sudden and leading the unwary into danger, they flourish in the stagnant and marshy air of the courts.

They are made welcome at the courts, where people are amused by them without respecting them. No one troubles to inquire the genuineness of their titles of nobility, any more than to ask for the marriage certificates of the ladies who pass as their wives, or for evidence of the virginity of the girls they may bring along. Whoever can give pleasure, and relieve even for an hour that boredom which is the most deadly of all the sicknesses of a court, is sure to be a welcome guest. They are tolerated, as a man tolerates a courtesan who amuses him and does not rob him too impudently. Sometimes an artist or a swindler will have to put up (as had Mozart) with a kick in the behind from a princely boot; sometimes they find their way from the ballroom to the prison, and even, like Afflisio, the manager of the imperial theatre, to the galleys. The cleverest among them feather their nests; become tax-collectors, *souteneurs*, or even, as complaisant husbands of court whores, genuine noblemen and barons. But for the most part they find it wiser not to wait until the roast burns, for their whole charm lies in their novelty and their incognito. If they turn up the corners of the cards too obviously, if they dip their hands too deep into people's pockets, if they make themselves at home too long in any one court, it may well happen that someone will tear the cloak from their shoulders and disclose the mark of the branding iron or the scar left by the lash. Frequent change of air is necessary to save them from the hangman's noose. That is why they are continually on the move across Europe, commercial travellers of a peculiar kind, gypsies who pitch their moving tents in palace after palace. Thus it is that throughout the eighteenth century a rotation of the same figures proceeds from Madrid to St Petersburg, from Amsterdam to Pozsony, from Paris to Naples. At first one is inclined to think it is no more than a lucky chance that, at every gaming table and at all the petty courts one after another, Casanova should encounter the same rogues, Talvis, Afflisio, Schwerin, and Saint-Germain; but the adept knows that such perpetual wanderings denote flight rather than a round of amusements.

There is a genuine freemasonry among these rogues. When they meet as old acquaintances, one of them will hold the ladder for another, and one of them will vouch for another. They exchange wives, coats, names; and there is only one thing which each of them keeps for himself—his own special profession. Parasites of the courts, these actors, dancers, musicians, adventurers, harlots, and alchemists, form, in conjunction with the Jesuits and the Jews, the only International that as yet exists in the world of the eighteenth century; the nobility is rootless, fixed to this court or to that; and the bourgeoisie is dull, immobile, not yet emancipated. But the rabble of freebooters, without flag and without fatherland, moves on freely from one country to another and rubs shoulders with all classes. With their appearance, a new age dawns, and a new method of exploitation. They are not like the footpads of old, who plundered the defenceless, not like the highwaymen who, pistol in hand, robbed the travellers in coaches; their art is a subtler one. For them, a ready wit has replaced the cudgel, and a calculated impudence proves more effective than the bravado of the old-style robber. Their success is the outcome of a knowledge of psychology. These new cutpurses have sworn alliance with cosmopolitanism and good manners. They rob their victims with the aid of marked cards and forged bills of exchange.

They are of the same race as the bold fellows who sailed to the Indies in the earlier days, who ruffled it as free companions, who would never be content to earn their livelihood in a humdrum civic fashion, but preferred to take big risks on the chance of filling their pockets at one blow. Now the method has changed, and therewith its physiognomy. The new adventurers have not the rough hands, the sodden faces, the coarse manners of those earlier captains; they have rings on their delicately kept fingers, and their heads are adorned with powdered wigs. They use a modish *lorgnon*, they walk like dancing masters, articulate like actors, mouth wise sayings like philosophers. With imperturbable visage, they cheat at cards; and with a patter of witty conversation, they persuade women to pay them a long price for love philtres and false jewels.

Beyond question, there is something attractive about them one and all; their wit and their psychological insight make them interesting; and some of them deserve to be named geniuses. The second half of the eighteenth century was their heroic period, their golden age. Just as earlier, under Louis XV, the French poets formed a brilliant pleiad, and just as later in Germany a brilliant group of creative writers made the name of Weimar ever memorable, so do the figures of these magnificent swindlers and immortal adventurers brilliantly characterize this particular period of European history. Ere long they are not content with dipping their hands into princely pockets; their ambition is to spin the roulette board of universal history. Instead of serving, they wish to make others serve them, with the result that the activity of adventurers has set its stamp upon the eighteenth century. John Law, an Irish wanderer, convulses the French currency with his *assignats*. D'Eon, passing for a man, but one whose sex is as dubious as his reputation, guides international policy. A little round-headed fellow, Baron Neuhof by name, becomes king of Corsica for a time, is later an inmate of debtors' prisons in various capitals, and dies in London as a pensioner in a debtors' prison. Cagliostro, a Sicilian peasant lad, who has never learned to read and write properly, has Paris at his feet, and fashions out of the famous necklace a halter which puts an end to monarchy. Trenck (the most tragic figure of them all, seeing that though an adventurer he was not devoid of true nobility) sports a red cap, plays the hero of freedom—and perishes on the guillotine. Saint-Germain has the king of France at his beck and call, and yet we are still puzzled concerning the mystery of his birth. One and all, these adventurers have more power than men born to power; they stimulate the fancy and arouse the attention of the whole world; they humbug the learned, lead women astray, plunder the rich, pull the strings of the political marionettes. Last and not worst among them comes our Giacomo Casanova, the historian of the guild, who describes them all when he describes himself, rounding off the story of these never-to-be-forgotten men with a hundred deeds and adventures of his own. Every one of them is more famous than the authors, more influential than the statesmen of their day; for a brief time they are the masters of a world already doomed to perish.

For the heroic age of the adventurers lasted no more than thirty or forty years. Then the stage on which they played was destroyed by the most finished of their type, by the most brilliant genius of them all, by the arch-adventurer, Napoleon. The characteristic of genius is that it does in real earnest that which talent does only as play-acting; that it is not content with make-believe, but demands the whole world as a stage for creative activities When Bonaparte, the impoverished little Corsican, calls himself Napoleon, this is not that he may, like Casanova-Seingalt, or like Balsamo-Cagliostro, hide his bourgeois origin behind a mask of nobility; he is putting forward a masterful claim to superiority, is seizing triumph as his right, instead of endeavouring to snatch it by craft. With Napoleon, adventurer of genius among a crowd of adventurers who had merely talent, the adventurer comes out of the ante-room of princes to seat himself on the imperial throne; and sets for a brief hour the most splendid of all crowns, the crown of Europe, upon his head.

TRAINING AND TALENTS

He is said to be a man of letters, but to have an
intelligence rich in cabals; it is reported that he
has been in England and in France, has gained
inexcusable advantages at the cost of knights and
ladies, for it has ever been his way to live at
others' expense, and to get the better of the credulous.
If we examine the aforesaid Casanova, we
see in him unbelief, fraud, unchastity, and
voluptuousness, assembled in an alarming way.

SECRET REPORT OF THE
VENETIAN INQUISITION, 1775

CASANOVA never denies having been an adventurer. On the contrary, he is proud of having
been the flat-catcher rather than the flat, the shearer
rather than the shorn, in a world where, as the old
adage says, people want to be fooled. One thing,
however, he strongly objects to. You must not con-
found him with commonplace knaves, jailbirds and
brethren of the halter, who pick pockets in a rough
and commonplace fashion, instead of elegantly charming money out of the hands of the stupid. In the
memoirs, he is always careful to shake the dust from

his cloak when he has had to acknowledge meeting (and, in truth, making common cause) with the card-sharpers Afflisio or Talvis—for although, as rogues, they have to meet on the same plane, they come from different worlds. He, Casanova, is from an upper world, a cultured world; they come from below, from nowhere. Casanova thus resembles the some-time student, Schiller's sententious robber-captain, Karl Moor, who despises his confederates Spiegel-berg and Schufterle because they have a positive liking for their rough and bloody trade; to which he has taken from a misguided enthusiasm, in order to revenge himself for the baseness of the world. In the same way Casanova always energetically dissociates himself from the mob of common rogues, in whose figures the splendid, the distinguished profession of adventurer forfeits its splendour and its distinction. Nay, verily, our friend Giacomo would have us regard as noble that which the ordinary citizen looks on as dishonourable, and the stickler for propriety as re-volting. He finds a philosophical justification for the adventurer's career. Far from being an unsavoury business, it is, for him, a fine art. According to him, for the philosopher here below there is no other moral duty than to amuse himself to the top of his bent at the cost of the blockheads, to dupe the vain, cheat the simple, relieve misers of their superfluous wealth, make cuckolds of the husbands—in a word, play the part of envoy of divine justice and punish all the follies of this world. Thus, for him, fraud is not merely a fine art, but a supreme moral duty; and, as a worthy outlaw, he practises it with an excellent conscience and incomparable self-satisfaction.

If we are to believe Casanova, he did not become an adventurer simply because he was short of money and had inherited a slothful disposition, but from temperament, fired by genius. Having had a talent for acting handed down to him by his father and his mother, he made the whole world into his stage, of which Europe was the centre. For him, as for Til Eulenspiegel of old, to humbug his fellows, to make fools of them, came by nature, and he could not live except in a carnival atmosphere of dominoes and jesting. Again and again, a hundred times over, he had a chance of entering some respectable occupation, of settling down in a warm and well lined nest; no temptation of this kind could induce him to make himself at home in a respectable occupation. If you were to offer him millions, high office and a dignified position, he would not accept them; he wished always to remain in his own element. He had good reason, therefore, for the pride with which he distinguishes himself from other adventurers. He is urged on to his madcap exploits, not by desperation, but by sheer delight in what he is doing. Furthermore, it is true enough that he did not originate like Cagliostro from a foul country hovel, or like Count Saint-Germain from utterly unknown beginnings which we may assume to have been equally malodorous. Messer Casanova was certainly born in lawful wedlock, and from a family in tolerably good repute. His mother, nicknamed *La Buranella*, was a famous cantatrice, who was acclaimed in all the opera-houses of Europe, and ultimately secured a permanent appointment at the court theatre in Dresden. His brother Giambattista's name is mentioned in every history of art as a noted pupil of Raphael Mengs, who was still regarded as a great artist at the close of the eighteenth century. This youngest Casanova's battle canvases can be seen in the leading galleries. The second son, Francisco, was likewise a painter of considerable renown. Giacomo's other relatives pursued dignified professions, that of lawyer, priest, and the like.

We see, then, that our Casanova did not come from the gutter, but sprang from the same artistic and variegated stratum of the burgher class as Mozart and Beethoven. Like them, he had had the advantage of an excellent general education. Having the gift of tongues he was able, amid all the scrapes of his youth and despite his premature amorous escapades, to learn Latin, Greek, French, and Hebrew, with a little

Spanish and English thrown in—although for thirty years the German language remained outside his ken. He excelled in mathematics no less than in philosophy. He was a competent theologian, preaching his first sermon in a Venetian church when he was not yet sixteen years old. As a violinist, he earned his daily bread for a whole year in the San Samuele theatre. When he was eighteen, so runs the tale, he became doctor of laws at the University of Padua—though down to the present day the Casanovists are still disputing whether the degree was genuine or spurious. This much is certain, that he must have had many advantages of a university education, for he was well informed in chemistry, medicine, history, philosophy, literature, and, above all, in the more lucrative (because more perplexing) sciences of astrology and alchemy. In addition, the handsome, nimble young fellow early became skilled in all the less intellectual arts that were then proper to a gentleman, such as dancing, fencing, riding, and card playing. If we add to these acquirements that he had an amazingly good memory, so that in all his life he never forgot a face, and never failed in the ability to recall anything he had heard, read, uttered, or seen, we have the picture of a man with quite exceptional endowments: almost a savant, almost a poet, almost a philosopher, almost a gentleman.

But this "almost" was for Casanova the heel of Achilles. He was almost everything: a poet and yet not wholly one, a thief and yet not a professional one. He strove hard to qualify for the highest intellectual rank, and strove hard to qualify for the galleys; yet he never succeeded in attaining perfection. As universal dilettante, indeed, he was perfect, knowing an incredible amount of all the arts and all the sciences; but he lacked one thing, and this lack made it impossible for him to become truly productive. He lacked will, resolution, patience. Let him study the books of some specialty for a year, and you will find no better jurist, no more brilliant historian. He might become a professor of any science, so quickly and accurately does his brain work. But he has no taste for thoroughness. A confirmed gamester, he finds serious application impossible; intoxicated with the wine of life, he revolts against commonplace perseverance. He never wants to be anything, for he is content to seem to be everything. The semblance suffices him, since it deceives his fellows, to cheat whom is an inexhaustible delight. Experience has taught him that a little learning is enough. In any domain, no matter what, where he has the first elements of knowledge, a splendid assistant springs to his aid—his stupendous impudence, his unchallengeable self-confidence, his unswerving courage.

Whatever Casanova undertakes, he never admits that he is a novice in the enterprise. He promptly assumes the manners of an expert, plays the swindler or cardsharper to perfection, and can almost always extract himself from a tangle. In Paris, Cardinal de Bernis asks him whether he knows anything about lotteries. He is as ignorant of them as a babe unborn, but it need hardly be said that he answers glibly in the affirmative, appears before a committee and, with his unrivalled gift of the gab, unrolls financial schemes as if he had been a bank manager for the last twenty years. He is in Valencia when the text of an Italian opera is missing. Casanova sits down and writes one offhand. Beyond a doubt if he had been asked to write the music as well as the libretto, he would have put together something out of the old operas. In Russia, he presents himself to Catherine the Great as a reformer of the calendar and a learned astronomer. In Courland, a no less ready-made expert, he inspects the mines. Playing the chemist, he recommends to the republic of Venice a new method of dyeing silk. In Spain, he poses as a land reformer and a colonizer. He drafts for Emperor Joseph II an elaborate scheme to prevent usury. He writes comedies for the duke of Waldstein; constructs the tree of Diana and similar specimens of alchemist hocus-pocus for the Marchioness of Urfé; and he opens

Madame de Rumain's treasure chest with the key of Solomon. He buys shares for the French government. In Augsburg, he presents himself as the Portuguese ambassador; in France, he is by turns a manufacturer and the pimp who keeps the royal "deer park" supplied; in Bologna, he writes a pamphlet on medicine; in Trieste, he pens a history of Poland and translates the *Iliad* into *ottava rima*. He has the talent for doing anything in the world without making himself look ridiculous. If we glance through the list of his posthumous writings, we fancy that they must be those of a universal philosopher, of an encyclopaedist, of a new Leibnitz. Here is a long novel, side by side with the opera *Odysseus and Circe*, an attempt at doubling the cube, a political dialogue with Robespierre. If you had asked him to give a proof of the existence of God or to write a hymn in praise of chastity, he would not have hesitated for a moment.

Beyond question he was a man of splendid and most varied gifts. Conscientiously applied in any direction, whether to science, art, diplomacy, or business, they would have sufficed to achieve wonders. Casanova deliberately frittered away his talents upon the purposes of the fleeting moment; and he, who might have been anything, preferred to be nothing but free. "The idea of settling down was always repulsive to me, and a reasonable course of life never

came naturally to me." He cannot endure the pros-
pect of a fixed occupation, whether it be that of well-
paid manager of lotteries to His Most Christian
Majesty, or that of a manufacturer, or that of a fiddler, or that of author. Hardly has he seated himself
anywhere, when he gets bored by the daily routine,
trips forth from his cosy nook into the street, and
hastens to stake his all upon some new hazard. His
true profession, he is convinced, is to have no profession; to give all the arts and sciences a trial by turns,
and to change roles night after night like an actor in
a repertory theatre. Besides, why should he moor
himself anywhere? He does not want to have and to
hold. A man of impetuous passions, he wants, not
one life but a hundred. Since he is a devotee of freedom, since he only wishes to be assured of income
and amusement and the joys of love for the hour
that has just begun, since he never demands permanent security, he can laughingly dispense with home
and possessions, which are nothing more than ties.
Had they been written then, he would have approv-
ingly quoted the lines of Grillparzer:

> The thing thou holdest, has thee in its grip;
> And where thou rulest, art in truth a slave.

Casanova would never be the slave of anything or
anyone except chance, which does indeed handle

him rudely at times, but is surprisingly good to him as a rule. True to this mistress, he contemptuously rejects anything that could chain him fast, and is a free thinker in the most literal sense of the term. "My greatest treasure," he says proudly, "is that I am my own master, and have no dread of misfortune." A manly device, which ennobles him more than does his borrowed title of Chevalier de Seingalt. He pays no heed to what others may think of him, but leaps with charming recklessness over the moral hurdles with which they would fence him in, indifferent to the anger of those whom he leaves behind and to the wrath of those whose hedges he breaks down. As he speeds onward, he gets flying views of those who are engaged in fixed occupations; they seem to him ridiculous and contemptible. Nor is he impressed by the warlords, rattling their sabres, and yet yielding to the clamour of their generals. The learned are bookworms. The financiers sit anxiously watching their money-bags, and cannot sleep at night for fear lest their strongboxes should be rifled. No woman can hold him long in her arms; no ruler can persuade him to stay within the boundaries of any one country; no occupation can bind him for more than a brief space. In these matters, too, he breaks boldly out of the Leads in Venice, for he will rather risk his life than let it turn sour. All his talents, all his abilities, all his powers, all his courage, and all his genius, he will stake day after day on the table of fortune, his goddess. That is why his existence remains as mutable as running water, now appearing as a fountain sparkling in the sunshine, now as a cascade thundering down into a dark abyss. From a prince's table into prison, from the easy life of a spendthrift with money in his purse to that of a man who can only get food by pawning his coat, from seducer to *souteneur*, he moves with lightning speed; and through it all his spirits are mercurial, he is wanton in days of good fortune and equable in days of evil, always full of courage and confidence.

Courage, that is the keynote of Casanova's art of life; that is his gift of gifts. He does not try to ensure against disaster, but fearlessly risks his life. Among the thousands whose motto is "safety first," here is one who hazards all, and takes every chance. Well, we know that Dame Fortune smiles on the bold. She gives freehandedly to the idle and to the impudent where she is a niggard to the diligent; she prefers the impatient to the patient; and thus, upon this one man who is so immoderate in his demands, she showers more gifts than upon a whole generation of his contemporaries. She lifts him up and casts him down again, hurries him from land to land, gives him plenty of exercise. She sates him with women and fools him at the gaming table; she titillates him with passions, and cheats him with fulfilment. But she never forgets him, and never allows him to suffer from tedium. Herself indefatigable, she is a fit partner for this indefatigable man, perpetually finding him new opportunities and new ventures. Thus does his life become diversified, fantastical, kaleidoscopic, as hardly another in many centuries. Thus it is that he, who tells the story of his own life, he who never either was or wanted to be anything real, became an incomparable fabulist of existence—not, indeed, by his own will, but by that of life itself.

PHILOSOPHY OF
SUPERFICIALITY

I have lived as a philosopher.
CASANOVA'S LAST WORDS

WHEN LIFE flows in so broad a stream, this always implies a certain lack of spiritual depth. One who can dance on all waters with as much agility as Casanova, must needs be as light as a cork. Thus the essential characteristic of his greatly admired art of life is seen, when we look at it closely, to consist, not so much in a positive virtue or power, as in a negative, in his complete freedom from any kind of moral inhibition. If we take this morsel of humankind, through whom the warm blood of passion streams so ardently, and examine his psychological makeup, the first thing that strikes us is the utter lack of ethical organs. His heart, his lungs, his liver, his brain, his muscles, and especially his seminal vesicles—these, one and all, are vigorous and healthy. But when we turn to study the spiritual sphere, where moral peculiarities and convictions are

51

aggregated to form the mysterious tissue of character, we encounter absolute vacancy. There is nothing of this sort to be seen. With our acids and other solvents, with our scalpels and our microscopes, we shall still fail to detect in this otherwise sound organism even a trace of what is called conscience, of that spiritual superego which controls the impulses and senses. In so much firm, pleasure-loving flesh, we cannot find the merest trace of a moral nervous system. That explains the whole enigma of Casanova's subtle genius. Lucky man that he is, he has only sensuality, and lacks the first beginnings of a soul. Bound by no ties, having no fixed aim, restrained by no prudent considerations, he can move at a different tempo from his fellow mortals, who are burdened with moral scruples, who aim at an ethical goal, who are tied by notions of social responsibility. That is the secret of his unique impetus, of his incomparable energy.

He voyages round the world, and never wishes to set his foot on firm ground. He is independent of laws, a freebooter, a filibuster, urged onward by his uncontrolled passions. Like other outlaws, he ignores the conventions of society, disregards social regulations, has no respect for the unwritten laws of European morality. What other men regard as sacred or important, is to him not worth a trifle. If you try to explain to him the nature of a moral or conventional obligation, he will understand you just as little as a simpleton can understand metaphysics. Do you talk to him about love of country? He is a cosmopolitan who, during the seventy-three years of his life, has never had a sleeping-place of his own, and has lived at the sport of chance; he laughs at patriotism. *Ubi bene, ibi patria*; where he can best fill his pockets, and can most easily make his way into the bed of any woman for whom he takes a fancy; where he can most easily lead fools by the nose and enjoy all the comforts of life—there he stretches his legs out underneath the table and feels himself at home. Do you ask him to respect religion? He will profess any religion you like to name, will have himself circumcised or wear a Chinese pigtail, if the one or the other brings him the most trifling advantage; and all the time he will scoff at the new creed as heartily as he scoffs at the Roman Catholicism in which he was brought up. What does he need with a religion, he who believes only in the warm joys of this world? "Probably there is no life after death; but if there be, we shall find out in due course." Thus does he argue, nonchalantly, uninterestedly, disregarding subtleties. *Carpe diem*, make the most of the fleeting hour, suck it dry like a grape and fling away the skin; that is his maxim. Cling to the world of senses, to the visible, the tangible, pressing all the juice of pleasure you can out of each instant as it passes. There you have the whole of his philosophy, and it is one which enables him to throw aside with a contemptuous laugh all the bourgeois moral precepts based upon honour, respectability, duty, shame, and loyalty, which would hinder a man from giving free rein to his impulses.

Honour? What can honour mean to Casanova? He esteems it no more than did fat Falstaff, who said, truly enough, that honour cannot set an arm or a leg, or take away the grief of a wound. Casanova is like the worthy English member of parliament, who once remarked in the House that he was continually hearing of our obligations to posterity, but would very much like to know what posterity has done for us. Honour cannot be enjoyed, cannot be grasped; it serves only to interfere with the enjoyment by inter-posing duties and obligations. That is enough to show that regard for honour is superfluous, seeing that duty and obligation are to Casanova the most detestable things in the world. The only duty he knows is the duty of feeding his high-strung body full of pleasure, and of sharing that elixir of pleasure with the greatest possible number of women. He never troubles to ask, therefore, whether his own warm fragrant existence has for others a good or a bad, a sweet or a sour taste; whether they regard his conduct as honourable or dishonourable, as worthy or shameful.

Shame? What an extraordinary word, what an incomprehensible idea! There is no such word in his dictionary. With the frank indifference of a *lazzarone*, in the full gaze of the public, he cheerfully takes down his breeches, and, with a broad grin, displays his genital organs, cheerfully discloses what another would keep to himself even on the rack, boasts of his rogueries, makes a parade of his very failures, his blunders, his attacks of venereal disorder; and he does all this, not with the mien of one who feels impelled to trumpet the crude truth, as does Jean-Jacques Rousseau, fully aware that his hearers will be amazed and horrified. Casanova is frank and unconcerned because he is not equipped with the nerves that would have enabled him to recognize moral distinctions, because he has no sense-organ adapted to make him aware of moral considerations. If you were to reproach him for having cheated at cards, he would merely answer, astonished at your chiding: "Oh, yes, I did cheat; I was in want of money!" Should you berate him for seducing a woman, he would answer with a laugh: "I gave her a jolly good time!" He would never dream of offering any excuse for having charmed money out of the pockets of the credulous. On the contrary, in his memoirs he approves these misdeeds of his by cynically remarking: "Reason takes its revenge when one cheats a blockhead." He does not defend himself. He never repents. Instead of wearing sackcloth and ashes, instead of lamenting over a misspent life which is ending in abject poverty and dependence, the toothless old rogue writes with delicious impudence: "I should regard myself blameworthy if I were rich today. But I have nothing left, I have squandered all my possessions, and that is a great consolation to me."

He has laid up no treasure in heaven, has not refrained from indulging any of his passions out of regard for the dictates of morality or the welfare of his fellows; he has hoarded nothing, either for his own sake or for others'; and from his seventy years nothing is left to him save memories. Even these memories he would not hoard, but, to our good fortune, has squandered them on us. Surely, therefore, we should be the last to complain of his spendthrift ways.

To put Casanova's philosophy in a nutshell, it begins and ends with the admonition: "Live for this world, unconcernedly and spontaneously; do not allow yourself to be cheated by regard for another world (which may indeed exist, but whose existence is extremely doubtful), or by regard for posterity. Do not let finespun theories divert your attention from things close at hand; do not direct your endeavours towards a distant goal; follow the promptings of the moment. Foresight will cripple your activities here and now. Do not trouble your head with prudent considerations. Some strange deity has set us down in our seat at this gaming table of a world. If we wish to amuse ourselves there, we must accept the rules of the game, taking them as they are, without troubling to inquire whether they are good rules or bad."

In actual fact, never for a moment did Casanova waste his time in pondering the problem whether this world could have been or ought to have been different. "Love mankind, but love it as it is," he says in conversation with Voltaire. Do not try to play providence; leave that sort of thing to the creator of the world, who is responsible for it. Do not try to knead the old dough, for you will only soil your hands; it is much simpler, and far more agreeable, to pick out the raisins, daintily. One who thinks too much about others, forgets himself; one who devotes too much attention to watching the course of the world, paralyses his own limbs. It seems to Casanova quite in order that stupid folk should have a bad time. As for the clever ones, God does not help them, and it is their own business to help themselves. Since we have to live in a crossgrained world, where some wear silk stockings and drive in carriages, while others, with empty bellies, must go afoot and in rags, then, for a reasonably clever fellow, the obvious thing is to make sure that he will be one of the carriage-folk—seeing that a man lives for himself, and not for others. No doubt that sounds extremely selfish; and yet, how can a philosophy of enjoyment be anything but selfish, how can one be an epicurean unless one is indifferent to the welfare of society? He who has a passionate desire to live for his own sake is perfectly logical when he callously disregards the fate of others.

Indifferent to others, indifferent to the great problems which each new day brings to mankind, Casanova lives his three and seventy years in impudent self-satisfaction. If, with his keen eyes, he looks eagerly to right and to left, this is only because he is in search of amusement, and does not want to miss any chances. But he will never wax indignant, will never follow Job's example of propounding unseemly questions to God Almighty. With an amazing economy of feeling, he takes everything as it comes, without troubling to label it as good or evil. When O'Morphi, a little Flemish drab of Irish extraction, fifteen years old, a girl who sleeps on straw and is ready to sell her virginity for a ducat, becomes a fortnight later one of the mistresses of His Most Christian Majesty, has a palace in the Parc aux Cerfs, is loaded with jewels, and in due course marries a complaisant

58

nobleman; or when he himself, who was yesterday a poor fiddler in a Venetian suburb, suddenly finds himself the adopted son of a patrician, has money in his pocket and diamonds on his fingers—these things seem to him curious incidents, worth recording, but nothing to make a fuss about. That is the way of the world, unjust and incalculable. Since it will always be like this, always unjust, always incalculable, why rack your brains trying to discover a law of gravity? Life is a switchback, and such fantastic ups and downs are its commonplaces. Only fools and the avaricious try to play roulette on a system, thus depriving themselves of the true enjoyment of the game. The real gambler, in life as well as at the gaming table, finds the greatest of all charms in the incalculability of events. Use tooth and claw to secure the best for yourself, *voilà toute la sagesse*. Be a philosopher for your own good, not for the good of humanity. As interpreted by Casanova, this means that you are to be strong, covetous, ruthless, as you clutch the flying moments and make the most of them. For this convinced pagan, nothing but the actual moment counts. The next moment is uncertain. Never does he allow his pleasures to be interfered with by thinking of next time, for this present times makes up his whole world, the here and now which he can grasp with all his organs. "Life, be it happy or unhappy, fortunate or unfortunate, is the only good man possesses, and he who does not love life is unworthy of life." Only that which breathes, only that which meets pleasure with pleasure, only that which (skin to skin) sensuously responds to his hot caresses—this and only this seems, to our confirmed anti-metaphysician, truly real and interesting.

Thus Casanova's interest in the world is confined to the organic, to the human. Never in his life, as far as we can judge, did he contemplate the starry heavens. The beauties of nature left him cold. Flutter the pages of the sixteen volumes of his memoirs. You see a man with keen senses travelling through the most beautiful landscapes of Europe, from Posilipo to Toledo, from the Lake of Geneva to the Russian steppes; but you will never find any reference to the beauties of natural scenery. A dirty little wench in a soldiers' drinking booth seems to him more important than all the works of Michelangelo; and he finds a game of cards in a stuffy tavern more beautiful than a sunset at Sorrento. Scenery and architecture are sealed books to Casanova, since he lacks the organ which brings us into touch with the cosmos, since he has no soul. Fields and meadows glowing red at sunrise, dew-sprinkled, with the long shadows of the trees lying athwart them; for him they are but green surfaces, on which the peasants, stupid as their

own cattle, toil and sweat that their lords may have
gold in pouch. Bosquets and dark alleys, they are
some use certainly, for there a man can get out of
sight with a woman when he wishes to enjoy himself.
As for flowers, they are useful presents when you
want to catch a woman's fancy. But, having eyes
only for human beings, he is colour-blind to the aim-
less, the purposeless beauty of nature. For him, the
world consists exclusively of towns with their galleries
and their promenades, where the carriages drive up
and down in the evening; the haunts of lovely
women, places beset with coffee-houses in which one
can play faro and win money from the other guests;
places where there are opera-houses and brothels,
and where it is easy to find a bedfellow for the night;
places where there are good inns in which the cooks
poetize with sauces and ragouts, and make music
with white wine and red. Only the towns are the
world for this man of pleasure, since in them alone
can chance provide its manifold surprises, since
there alone is the incalculable room to work out its
infinitely numerous and entrancing variations.

Casanova loves towns for their thronging popula-
tions. In the towns are women as he enjoys them, in
the plurality which saves him from the risk of
monotony. Among towns, he likes best of all court
towns, towns where luxury is rife, for there the

voluptuous is sublimated into the artistic. Casanova, sensual though he be, is not a crude sensualist. An aria, beautifully sung, can charm him; a poem can captivate him; agreeable conversation warms his wine for him. To converse with clever men about books, or to listen to music while, in a box at the opera, he sits closely pressed against a fascinating woman; these intensify his joy in life. But we must not make any mistake here. Casanova's love for art is merely sportive, and never gets beyond the pleasure of a dilettante. For him, the spirit must serve life, since he will never live in order to serve the spirit. For him, therefore, art is nothing more than the finest and most subtle of aphrodisiacs; a means for stimulating the senses, for heightening enjoyment. It is a prelude to passion, a prelude that will enhance the subsequent joys of the flesh.

He will write a little poem, and will hand it, with a garter, to a lady whom he covets; he will recite some verses of Ariosto, to inflame her passion; with gentlemen, he will converse wittily about Voltaire and Montesquieu, that he may put himself on a good footing with them intellectually, and mask his designs on their purses. But this sensualist, a lazy southerner, never troubles himself about art or science when these demand pains and thoroughness, when they have to be pursued as ends in themselves and as disciplines having a worldwide significance. One who has no thought beyond amusement, he shuns depths because he is content with the surface of things, with the frothy and perfumed upper levels of existence, with chance flirtations. He is always enjoying himself as a dilettante, and that is why he is so light on the wing, can flit so easily from blossom to blossom. Just as Dürer's *Fortuna* speeds barefoot over the spinning earth, borne up by her pinions, wafted onward by any wind that blows, settling nowhere, faithful to none, so does Casanova skim over the surface of life, forming no ties, but changing ever. Change is for him "the salt of pleasure," and pleasure is the only meaning of the world.

Buoyant on the wing as a mayfly, empty as a soap-bubble, sparkling in the light of passing events, he flutters on his way. Can we say that he has a character at all, seeing that it varies from hour to hour, and has no substance we can grasp? What is Casanova at bottom? Is he good or evil? Is he an honest man or a knave, a hero or a rascal? He is one or the other as the hour may dictate. Chameleon-like he takes his colour from circumstances, changing as the background varies. When he is in funds, you will not find anywhere a more distinguished gentleman. With charming profusion, with a radiant grandeur, amiable as some great prelate and merry as a page, he scatters his money with both hands. "I was never one to trouble about thrift." Like a high-born patron, he invites casual strangers to dinner, presents them with jewelled snuffboxes and *rouleaux* of ducats, does everything he can to delight them. But if you meet Casanova when his pockets are empty, and when unpaid bills are accumulating, I would advise you to avoid playing cards with this *galantuomo*. He will be in the mood to cheat you at every turn, will get you to change forged notes for him, will trade off his mistress, will play you the most scurvy tricks. As undependable as a throw of the dice, he will today be the best and most entertaining companion in the world, and tomorrow a villainous footpad; on Monday he will pay court to a woman with all the delicacy of an Abelard, and on Tuesday he will play the pimp and sell her favours to anyone willing to give him a ten-pound note.

You cannot say that Casanova has either a good character or a bad one; he has no character at all. Character and spiritual substance are not among his attributes, any more than fins are proper to a mammal. His actions are neither moral nor immoral; they are simply amoral. Whatever he does is the reflex outcome of his physical makeup, and is quite uninfluenced by reason, logic, or ethical considerations. Let him catch sight of a woman, and all his pulses are beating; blindly he moves towards her under the urge of his temperament. When he comes across a gaming table, his hand is instantly in his pocket, and before he knows it he has staked his money. Do something that annoys him, and his fury has no bounds, his eyes flash, his cheeks flame, he clenches his fist and strikes out madly, charges *come un bue*, as his fellow countryman and brother adventurer Benvenuto Cellini says. It is absurd, therefore, to hold Casanova accountable for what he does. It is not he who acts, but the hot blood within him, and there is no "he" to cope with its elemental impulses. "I never have been and never shall be able to master myself." He does not reflect and he never looks forward. When he is in a tight place, some brilliant flash of insight will often get him out of the difficulty, but he never calculates, never tries to plan before difficulties come. He is too impatient for that. Read the memoirs, and you will see that all his decisive actions, ranging from absurd practical jokes to the most outrageous rascalities, were the outcome of explosions of caprice, and were never dictated by intelligent calculation. Impulsively, one day, he casts aside the *abate's* frock; on another occasion, when he is a soldier at the front, he sets spurs to his horse and canters over the lines in order to surrender to the enemy; he sets off for Russia or for Spain, following his nose, carrying no letters of recommendation, and without having troubled to ask himself why he is going or whither. All his decisions are like unexpected pistol shots, the fruit of a sudden whim, of a determination to escape from boredom. So unexpectedly do these impulses hurl him out of one situation into another, that he is often startled, and rubs his eyes in his surprise. Indeed, he has to thank his bold reliance upon casual promptings for the richness of his experience. One who acts logically, one who calculates every step, does not become an adventurer; and a careful strategist will never enjoy such wonderful chances.

Nothing, therefore, could be more fallacious than the way in which many of our imaginative writers who choose Casanova as a hero of a play or a novel depict him as endowed with a thoroughly alert intelligence, as being of a reflective type, as Faust and Mephistopheles rolled into one. All his impetus is the outcome of his failure to reflect, of his amoral heedlessness. Instil no more than a drop or two of sentimentality into his blood, burden him with self-knowledge and a sense of responsibility, and he will no longer be Casanova; drape him Byronically, add a conscience to the ingredients of which he is composed, and you will have an alien being. His essence is unreflection. Unreflectingly, he grasps at every toy that comes within his reach; at women, at pleasures, at other people's purses. In this, he is not driven by daimonic, by elemental forces; the only elemental force that drives Casanova has a commonplace name and a familiar, stupid countenance—is nothing other than boredom. Since he has an absolutely vacant mind, has no inner resources, he can only escape infinite boredom by an incessant recurrence of objective experiences; without the oxygen of adventure, he is suffocated. Hence his insatiable greed for whatever he has not yet had, for anything different from what he has known; hence his unappeasable hunger for new experiences. Having no inner source of productivity, he must unceasingly assimilate vital substance from without; but this voracious appetite is utterly different from the daimonic urge of the essentially masterful and acquisitive temperament—that of a Napoleon, who must add land to land and kingdom to kingdom, impelled by a thirst for infinity; or that of a Don Juan, who must seduce one woman after another, that he may know himself to be autocrat of another infinity, the world of woman. Casanova, who is nothing more than a pleasure seeker, does not traffic in such superlatives; he is merely on the lookout for a continuity of pleasure. He is not like the man of action, not like the man of the spirit, whom a fanatical illusion drives on towards a dangerous tension of feeling; he wants nothing more than the genial warmth of enjoyment, the sparkling delight of the game; adventures, adventures, adventures, ever varying; occupation for the ego, reinforcement of life. Above all, not to be alone; not to shiver in a frosty vacancy of solitude.

Look at Casanova when entertainment is lacking. Then, every sort of rest becomes to him a terrible unrest. He arrives at eventide in a strange town. Nothing will induce him to spend the last hours of the day in his room, communing with his thoughts, or reading a book. He snuffs the wind eagerly, to see if it brings with it any scent of amusement. In default of better, the chambermaid at the inn can help to keep him warm as he lies abed that night. Lounging at the bar, he will hold converse with chance comers; he will play faro with cardsharpers in any low gaming house; will spend the night with the most pitiful harlot rather than sleep alone: always the sense of inner vacancy drives him into converse with his fellows, for only through friction with other living creatures can his own vitality be kept up. Directly he is alone, he becomes one of the gloomiest, one of the most bored of men. We see this in his writings, the memoirs alone excepted. It is plain during the lonely years at Dux, where he speaks of boredom as "hell," as "the inferno which Dante forgot to describe." Just as a whipping-

top must be incessantly lashed if it is to be kept spinning, so Casanova needs an incessant spurring from
without. Like so many other adventurers, he is an
adventurer because of his lack of spiritual energy.

That is why, as soon as the natural tension of life
begins to flag, he has recourse to the artificial tension of gaming. At the gaming table he can find an
abbreviated recapitulation of the tension of life, artificial dangers and artificial rescues. The gaming
table is the asylum of all men of the fleeting hour,
the perpetual solace of the idle. At the gaming table,
he can enjoy a stormy ebb and flow of the feelings;
the empty seconds, the weary hours, are filled with
the titillation of anxiety, with shuddering expecta-
tion. Gambling, therefore, like nothing else in the
world with the doubtful exception of women, solaces
with spurious adventures the man who is weary of
himself, and serves better than anything else to
occupy one who has no inner resources and occupations. Never was any one more hopelessly subject to
the lure of the gaming table than Casanova. Just as
he cannot look on a woman without longing to possess her, so he cannot see money on a gaming table
without putting fingers into his pockets to take out
his own stake. Even when he recognizes in the man
keeping the bank a notorious plunderer, a colleague
in cardsharping, he will still hazard his last ducat,

knowing perfectly well that he will lose it. Casanova himself, beyond question—although the memoirs are chary of acknowledging that which police records place beyond dispute—was one of the cleverest card-sharpers of his day; and for all his skill in other forms of roguery, and his incidental earnings as a *souteneur*, cardsharping was his chief means of subsistence. Nothing, then, can show his obsession with the passion for gambling, nothing can manifest his craze for games of chance, more plainly than this, that, although he was himself a plunderer, he would continually allow himself to be plundered because he could not resist the gambler's lure. Just as a prostitute, whose money is earned laboriously enough, will hand over these hard-earned gains to her pimp simply in order to experience in actuality the pleasures she simulates in intercourse with her ordinary clients, so does Casanova disburse to past masters at the game the funds he has impudently filched from novices. Not once, but twenty times, a hundred times, does he lose on the turn of a card all that he has gained by arduous cheating. This is what stamps him as gambler in blood and bone, that he does not play in order to win (how tedious that would be!) but in order to play; just as he does not live in order to be rich, happy, and comfortable, but simply in order to live, being here likewise the born gambler.

He never looks for a final relief of tension. What he wants is perpetual tension, the unceasing alternation of red and black, of spades and diamonds. Only in these perpetual ups and downs does he find contentment for his nerves.

In ordinary life, as at the gaming table, he needs these gains and losses, the conquest and discarding of women, the contrast between poverty and riches, unending adventure. Inasmuch as even such a life as his, ceaselessly varying though it be like a moving picture on the screen, nevertheless has intervals, sudden breaks, sudden surprises, and sudden storms, he fills in these empty pauses with the artificial tension of the gaming table. Thanks to his mad ventures here, he is able to achieve the amazing oscillations of fortune, his swift ascents to the zenith, and his no less swift plunges to the nadir. Today his pockets are stuffed with gold, he is a grand seigneur, with two servants standing at the back of his coach; tomorrow he has had to sell his diamonds to a Jew, and even to pawn his breeches (this is not written in jest, but is literally true, for the pawn-ticket was found at Zurich). That is how our arch-adventurer likes to live, moving on from explosion to explosion of fortune and misfortune. Enjoying hazard for its own sake, again and again he stakes his life upon a cast. Ten times, in duels, he stood in the very jaws of death. A score of times he was in imminent danger of the penitentiary or the galleys. Millions passed into his hands and out again, and he never troubled to save. For the very reason that he gave himself thus unreservedly to the game of life, enjoying to the full every woman, every moment, every adventure; for that very reason, though he was to drag out his declining years as a poor pensioner in a strange land, he attained his highest aim—an infinite abundance of life.

HOMO EROTICUS

Seducer, say you? Nay, I was but there
When Nature, with her splendid witchery,
Began her work. Nor must you dub me false,
For I am ever thankful in my heart.

ARTHUR SCHNITZLER: CASANOVA'S RETURN TO VENICE

HE IS A DILETTANTE, and generally a second-rate one at that, in all the arts God has created: he writes lame verses and dull philosophical disquisitions; he can play the fiddle passably; and the best one can say of his conversation is that it shows an encyclopædic smattering. He may count as an expert in all the games of the devil's making, such as faro, biribi, dicing, dominoes, the confidence trick, alchemy, and diplomacy. But in the art of love, Casanova excels all his rivals. Here his manifold talents, which are fragmentary and botched for the most part, combine with a subtle chemistry to make of him the perfect erotist; in this matter, he is indisputably a genius of first rank. His physique is enough to show that he was designed for the service of Cytherea. Nature, parsimonious as a rule, has been free-handed here, equipping him liberally with sap, sensuality, vigour, and beauty; a man apt to delight women's hearts, a thoroughly masculine creature, strong and supple as steel, a well-tempered example of his sex, massive in mould, and yet admirable in form. You would make a big mistake were you to imagine Casanova, the conqueror of women, to have been of the delicate type of male beauty which is nowadays in vogue. This *bel uomo* is no ephebe; nothing of the sort! He is a stallion of a man, with the shoulders of the Farnese Hercules, the muscles of a Roman wrestler, the bronzed beauty of a gypsy lad, the impudence and audacity of a *condottiere*, and the sexual ardour of a satyr. His powers of resistance are stupendous. Four attacks of venereal disease, two doses of poison, a dozen sword thrusts, the terrible years passed in the Leads in Venice and in pestilential Spanish jails, hurried journeys from Sicilian heats to the frosts of Muscovy—none of these things abate his phallic energy by a jot. No matter when or where, the merest spark from a woman's eyes, the first intimation of a woman's nearness, suffices to set his invincible sexuality aflame. For a busy quarter of a century he is invariably the *Messer Sempre Pronto*, the Mr Ever Ready, of the Italian farces, and up till the age of forty knows only by hearsay of that distressing fiasco which Stendhal, in his treatise *De l'amour*, thinks important enough to discuss in a supplementary section. A body that is never weary when appetite calls, an appetite which never fails, a passion which no extravagance can impoverish, a gambler's impulse that shrinks from no hazard—rarely indeed has nature bestowed upon any master so perfectly stringed and sensitive a bodily instrument, so splendid a *viola d'amore* for playing all the tunes of love. In any and every profession, for perfect mastery there is requisite, not only inborn talent, but also incessant concentration upon the pursuit. There must be an unswerving devotion to the chosen occupation, complete absorption in some particular direction; through that alone can absolute proficiency be secured. As the musician cultivates music, as the poet gives himself up to writing of verses or the miser to the hoarding of money, as the fanatic for sport throws everything else aside in his passion to break the record, an amorist who is to outdo all others must regard the wooing, the coveting, and the possession of woman as the most important, nay as the only, good in the world. The passions are jealous one of another, and for this reason he must have nothing to do with any other passion than that of love, must find therein the whole meaning of the

world. Casanova, fickle though he be, remains constant in his passion for woman. Offer him the doge's
ring of Venice, all the wealth of the Fuggers, a
patent of nobility, a house and a comfortable
appointment, fame as a general or an author; he will
contemptuously throw aside these worthless trifles to
hurl himself into the chase of some woman he has
not yet possessed, to enjoy her feminine aroma, the
delicious thrill of certain-uncertainty that she will
yield to him in the end. Everything else the world
can promise—honour, office and dignity, wealth,
any pleasure you like to name—he will disregard for
the sake of a love adventure, and even for the barest
possibility of such. He does not need to be positively
in love; the mere inkling that a love adventure is at
hand is enough to arouse anticipatory delight.

Let me give one example out of a hundred, that of
the episode which you will find at the beginning of
the second volume, when Casanova is rushing to
Naples on important business. At the inn where he
has halted for a brief space, he catches sight of a
pretty woman in a neighbouring room, in a
stranger's bed (that of a Hungarian captain). Nay,
what makes the matter more absurd is that he does
not yet know whether she is pretty or not, for she is
hidden under the bedclothes. He has merely heard
laughter, a young woman's laughter, and thereupon

his nostrils quiver. He knows nothing about her, whether she is attractive or the reverse, likely to be compliant or not, whether she is a possible conquest at all. Nevertheless he casts aside all his other plans, sends his horses back to the stable, and remains in Parma, merely because this off-chance of a love adventure has turned his head.

Thus does Casanova act after his kind anywhere and everywhere. By day or by night, in the morning or in the evening, he will commit any folly in the hope of spending an hour with an unknown woman. Where he covets, he grudges no price; where he wishes to conquer, he brooks no resistance. Wishing to see a woman once more, a German burgomaster's lady of whom he does not even know whether she can make him happy, he forces his way, in Cologne, into a company where he has not been invited, where he knows himself to be unwelcome, and has to accept a rating from the host and to endure the derision of the other guests. But what does the rutting stallion care for the blows of the whip that are rained on him? Casanova will cheerfully spend the whole night in a damp cellar, will endure cold and hunger and the company of rats uncomplainingly, for the chance that when dawn comes he will be rewarded by an hour of not overcomfortable amorous dalliance. He will, ever and again, risk sword thrusts, pistol shots, invectives, extortions, disease, humiliations—and for what? Not, as would be comprehensible enough, for an Anadyomene, for the pearl of womanhood, infinitely worthy of a man's love. He will risk all these things for Mistress Everywoman, for Mistress Anybody, simply because she is a woman, because she is a member of the opposite, the coveted, sex. Every pimp, every *souteneur*, can plunder this famous seducer; every complaisant husband or easygoing brother can involve him in the most discreditable affairs—provided his senses are stimulated. And when are they not stimulated? When is Casanova's erotic thirst fully quenched? *Semper novarum rerum cupidus*, always eager for some new thing, always questing after new prey, his lusts are incessantly aquiver for the unknown. A town without a love adventure is no town for him; the world without women is not a world. Just as his lungs need air, and his muscles need alternation of movement and repose, so does this virile body of his need the recurrent tensions and discharges of amorous embraces. Not for a month, not for a week, scarcely even for a day, can he feel at ease without women. In Casanova's vernacular, abstinence means, very simply, dullness and boredom.

Since he has so gargantuan an appetite, and since he satisfies it so persistently, we can hardly be surprised to find that the quality of his feminine provision is not always of the best. So champion a sensualist cannot afford to be fastidious; he cannot be an epicure, and must be content with the role of glutton. Consequently, it is no particular recommendation to a woman that she has been one of Casanova's innumerable mistresses. She need not have been a Helen of Troy, nor yet a chaste virgin, nor yet remarkably witty or wellbred or attractive, in order to enjoy the privilege of this gentleman's embraces. Enough for him, generally speaking, that she should be woman, vagina, his polar opposite in matters of sex, formed by nature to enable him to discharge his libido. Beauty, shrewdness, tenderness—no doubt these are agreeable accessories, but altogether subsidiary to the main point, sheer femininity; femininity, incorporated in a perpetually new shape, is all that Casanova desires.

You must rid yourself of any romantic or aesthetic notions concerning this extensive Parc aux Cerfs. Casanova's collection, like that of any professional amorist (perforce undiscriminating), is of unequal quality, and is anything but a gallery of beauty. You will certainly find there some sweet and tender girls, such as might have been painted by Casanova's fellow-countrymen Guido Reni and Raphael; others might have been limned by Rubens, or sketched by Boucher upon silk fans: but side by side with these you will find English streetwalkers, whose hard and impudent faces only the pencil of a Hogarth could have drawn; hideous old witches who might have graced the canvases of Goya; poxy drabs in the style of Toulouse-Lautrec; rough peasant-women and servant-girls such as Breughel might have painted—a medley of beauty and foulness, wit and vulgarity, a chance assembly at a fair, thrown together haphazard without assortment or choice.

For when his passions run away with him, this pan-eroticist has coarse nerves, and his fancy wanders into strange and devious paths. One who is ever at the mercy of his amorous impulses knows no prefer-ences. He pounces on the first comer; fishes in all waters, be they clean or dirty, be they fenced or un-fenced. This boundless and reckless eroticism knows nothing of the restrictions imposed by morality or good taste, by station or by age; it knows nothing of above or below, of too early or too late. Many of the objects of Casanova's passion are so young that in our stricter times his indulgence would certainly have brought down on him the heavy hand of the law; and others are women well advanced in years, including that septuagenarian ruin, the Marchioness of Urfé—assuredly the most preposterous love affair which ever a man has shamelessly recorded for the informa-tion of posterity. This most unclassical *Walpurgisnacht* ranges through all countries and all classes. Delicate girls, in the shuddering thrill of their first shame; distinguished ladies wearing priceless lace and resplendent with jewels; the scum of brothels; randy old women—all join hands in this witches' dance. The niece replaces the aunt, the daughter the mother, in the still-warm bed; procuresses give Casanova their own daughters, and husbands make it easy for him to possess their wives; soldiers' wenches and ladies of rank and station enjoy the pleasure of his embraces on the same night. You must not think it possible to depict the love adventures of Casanova after the graceful manner of eighteenth century pastoral etchings. You must, for once, have the courage to contemplate undiscriminating eroticism in all its crude contradictions, in its unmistakable realism, as the pandemonium of masculine sensuality.

Such a lust as Casanova's has no exceptions. It is lured equally by the abstruse and by the everyday; there is no anomaly which does not inflame it, nor any absurdity which can chill it. Lousy beds, dirty linen, offensive odours, comradeship with pimps, the presence of spectators, extortion, the diseases that attend indiscriminate venery, are inconsiderable trifles for this divine bull who, like the second Jupiter, wishes to embrace Europa, to clasp the whole world of woman in his arms, to sate his almost maniacal lust. But in one respect, his passions are scrupulously masculine. Stormy as is the raging torrent of his blood, it never flows outside the natural channel. Casanova's impulses are exclusively directed towards members of the other sex. He loathes contact with a castrato, and angrily whips a Ganymede out of his path. Despite all his vagaries, he remains constant to the world of women. But within this world his ardour knows no limits.

That is what gives Casanova his unprecedented power over women, that is what makes him irresistible—the Pan-like power of his rushing impetus, the elemental force of his sexual appetite. The hidden passion in women's own blood responds to this fierce passion of the male animal, to the tremendous ardour of the opposite sex. They let him take possession of them because he is fully possessed by them; they fall to him because he has fallen to them—and not so much to the one woman in the case, as to the plurality of women, to the universal femininity in the particular woman of the moment, to the opposite pole of his own sex. Intuitively they feel that here at length they have encountered one to whom nothing is more important than woman. He is not like nearly all other men, wearied by affairs and duties; now listless and husbandly, now eager and ardent; his wooing no more than a secondary and occasional matter. He assails them with the torrential might of his nature; he does not spare, he spends; he does not hesitate, does not pick and choose. In very truth, he gives himself to the uttermost, to the last drop of lust in his body, to the last ducat in his purse; always and unhesitatingly he is ready to sacrifice everything else to a woman because she is a woman, and at the moment can quench his thirst for woman.

To Casanova, the first and last word of enjoyment, and all enjoyment that lies between, is to see women happy, amazed with delight, rapturous, laughing, carried out of themselves. As long as he has money left, he lavishes presents on the woman of his momentary choice, flatters her vanity with luxurious trifles, loves to deck her out splendidly, loves to wrap her in costly laces before he unclothes her that he may enjoy her nakedness, loves to surprise her with gifts more expensive than she has ever dreamed of, loves to overwhelm her with the tokens of his extravagant passion. He is like one of the gods of Hellas, a bounteous Zeus, showering on his beloved the golden rain of his ardent passion. In this, too, he resembles Zeus, that thereafter he speedily vanishes into the clouds. "I have loved women madly, but I have always preferred freedom even to them." This increases his attraction, for the stormy phenomena of his appearance and disappearance enshrine him in their memory as something unwonted, which has brought them rapturous delight, so that association with him is never staled by habit.

Every one of these women feels that Casanova would be impossible as a husband, as a faithful Céladon; but as a lover, as a god of a passing night, they will never forget him. Though he forsakes them one and all, none of them would have had him different from what he was. Casanova, therefore, need only be himself, faithful to the unfaithfulness of his passion, and he will win every woman. A man such as this has no need to wear false colours, to pretend to be other than he is; he need not devise lyrical arts of seduction. Casanova need merely let his frank passion run its course, and this does the wooing for him. It is vain, therefore, for timid youths to devour the sixteen volumes of his *Ars Amandi*, in the hope of learning the master's secret. The craft of seduction can be no more learned from books than the writing of poetry. There is nothing to be learned from Casanova; there is no peculiar Casanova-trick, no Casanova technique of conquest and taming. His only secret is the straightforwardness of his desire, the elemental onslaught of his passionate nature.

I said just now "straightforward," but I might just as well have said "upright" or "honest"—astonishing words to apply to Casanova. No matter; though at the gaming table he has no scruple about using marked

cards, and though in any other field than love he is
the most accomplished of cheats, where love is concerned we must admit that he shows a straightforward
honesty of his own kind. Casanova's relationship to
women is truly honourable, because purely passionate, purely sensual. It may seem deplorable, but it is
true that insincerity in love makes its first appearance
with the intermingling of higher feelings. The body,
stupid worthy fellow that he is, does not lie; he never
intensifies his appetites beyond the naturally attainable.
Not until intellect and sentiment come to play their
part in the game, not until their soaring pinions are
at work, does passion become exaggerated, and therefore false, introducing fancied eternities into our
earthly relations. It is easy, therefore, for Casanova,
who never speaks idly of transcending the realm of the
bodily, to keep his promises; for, supplied from the
well-stored magazine of his sensuality, he exchanges
pleasure for pleasure, the bodily for the bodily, and
never runs into debt in the spiritual sphere.

That is why the women who have passed the night
with Casanova do not feel that they have been
cheated of platonic expectations. For the very reason
that he has never demanded from them any other
raptures than the orgasms of the flesh, for the very
reason that he has never made any pretence of an
eternity of sentiment, there will be no subsequent

phase of disillusionment. You have every right, if you wish, to describe such eroticism as love of the baser sort, as purely sexual, unspiritual, and animal; but you must not dispute its straightforwardness, its honesty. Surely this braggart, with his frank desire for possession, deals more honestly, deals better, with women than do the romanticist enthusiasts, the "great lovers," like (to give one example) the sensual-supersensual wooer Faust, who, in his extravagance, swears by sun and moon and stars, calls God and the universe to witness the nobility of his feelings for Gretchen, in order (as Mephistopheles has long foreseen) to end these high flights in a thoroughly Casanovese fashion, and, in the most earthly manner possible, to rob the poor fourteen-year-old girl of the treasure of her virginity. The path of a Goethe or a Byron is strewn with feminine wreckage. Men of a higher, a more cosmic nature, lift their companions to such sublime levels that the poor women, while unable to adapt themselves permanently to this stellar atmosphere, are unable, thereafter, to readapt themselves satisfactorily to their earthly habitat. Casanova's flash of earthly passion, on the other hand, does very little harm to their souls. He is not responsible for any shipwrecks, for any outbreaks of despair. He has made a great many women happy, but has made no women hysterical. From the episode of sensual adventure, they return undamaged to everyday life, to their husbands, or to other lovers, as the case may be. Not one of them commits suicide, or falls into a decline. Their internal equilibrium has never been disturbed, for Casanova's unambiguous and radically healthy passion has never touched the mainspring of their destiny. He has blown athwart them like a tropical hurricane, and after he has passed they will bloom in a more ardent sensuality. He has made them glow without singeing them; has conquered them without destroying them; has seduced them without corrupting them. Precisely because his erotic assault has been confined to the resistant tissues of the epidermis, and has never reached the vulnerable depths of the soul, his conquests never lead to catastrophes. Consequently, there is nothing daimonic about Casanova as a lover; he never brings tragedy into a woman's life. In the drama of love, the world's stage knows no more brilliant an episodist than he, but he is nothing more than an episodist.

Recognizing the utter lack of spirituality in Casanova's love adventures, we cannot fail to ask ourselves whether this libido which is purely physical, which is inflamed by the mere rustling of a woman's petticoat, is entitled to the name of love. Certainly not in a sense which would put Casanova, *homo eroticus vel eroticissimus*, in the same category with Werther or Saint-Preux, the immortal lovers. The sense of spiritual exuberance aroused by the sight of the beloved, a feeling akin to piety, which makes the lover regard his beloved as of one nature with the universe and with God, this ecstatic expansion of the soul under the influence of Eros, remains unknown to Casanova from the first day to the last. Nothing that he has ever written, no letter, no verses, betrays the existence in him of any amatory sentiments beyond those directly related to physical possession; and it is doubtful whether we can ascribe to him the faculty of true passion. For this *amour passion*, as Stendhal terms it, is, by its invariable uniqueness, incompatible with any such diurnal ordinariness; it is necessarily of rare occurrence, the outcome of a prolonged storing of the sensibilities, which are at length, like a lightning flash, discharged on the beloved object. There is no such thrift about Casanova. He squanders his ardours too often, relieves his tensions too frequently, to be capable of such high intensities of discharge. His passion, flowing away at the purely erotic level, knows nothing of the ecstasy of uniqueness. We need have no anxiety, therefore, when he seems reduced to despair because Henriette or the beautiful Portuguese lady has left him. We know that he will not blow out his brains; nor are we surprised

to find him, a day or two later, amusing himself in
the first convenient brothel. If the nun C. C. is
unable to come over from Murano, and the lay-sis-
ter M. M. arrives in her place, Casanova is speedily
consoled. After all, one woman is as good as
another! It soon becomes plain to us that, as an
arch-erotist, Casanova was never really in love with
anyone of the innumerable women he possessed. He
was in love with the plurality, with the incessant
variations, with the multiplicity of love adventures.

He himself made a dangerous admission when he
said: "Already I realized obscurely that love is nothing beyond a more or less lively curiosity." That is
all. He is curious. He wants to repeat his experiences
again and again, and always with a different woman.
It is not the individual that stimulates him, but the
variation, the new and ever new combination upon
Eros's inexhaustible chessboard. His taking and leaving is as simple and natural a function as inspiration
and expiration. That is why Casanova, as an artist,
was never able to make any one of his thousand
women a really lifelike figure to us. His descriptions
of them arouse a suspicion that he never troubled to
look his mistress lovingly in the face, but was content
to regard her in *certo punto*. What rouses him, what
"inflames" him, is always the same. A true southerner, he is interested in the grossly sensual, in

"country matters," in a woman's most obviously sexual characteristics. Again and again, till we grow weary of the iteration, he describes "alabaster breasts," "divine hemispheres," "the figure of a Juno"; and again and again he refers to the chance disclosure of "more intimate charms"; all the things that a lad in his salad days gets excited about in a servant wench. Thus, of the countless Henriettes, Irenes, Babettes, Mariuccias, Ermelines, Marcolinas, Ignazias, Lucies, Esthers, Saras, and Claras (one might almost write every name that has been given to a woman), little remains beyond a flesh-coloured jelly of voluptuous feminine bodies, a bacchantic medley of figures, functions, and enthusiasms—reminding us of the musings of a man who wakes in the morning with a sore head, and finds it difficult to recall where and with what boon companions he got drunk overnight. Of all the women he describes, not a single one moves before us vividly in the body, to say nothing of the soul. He has enjoyed them only skin-deep, has known them exclusively in the flesh.

Thus the accurate yard-stick of art discloses to us even more surely than life itself how immense a difference there is between mere eroticism and love in the true sense of the term; between that which wins all and retains nothing, and that which achieves little but by spiritual power makes the transient durable.

One single experience of Stendhal's (in truth, no hero in the field of love) contains, through sublimation, more spiritual substance than three thousand nights of Casanova's. As for the possibilities of love's most blissful spiritual ecstasies, Casanova's sixteen volumes give us less of an inkling of them than the briefest of Goethe's lyrics. Casanova's memoirs, therefore, regarded from the upland, are seen to be a statistical work of reference rather than a romance, the history of a campaign rather than a work of creative authorship; they are a *codex eroticus*, an occidental Kama Sutra, an Odyssey of the wanderings of the flesh, an Iliad of the eternal masculine rut for the eternal Helen. Their value depends upon quantity, not quality; upon multiformity, and not upon spiritual significance.

For the very reason that his sexual experiences were so multifarious, for the very reason that his physical potency was so unexampled, to our world, which is for the most part only interested in "records" and rarely measures spiritual capacity, Giacomo Casanova has become symbolic as phallic conqueror, has become proverbial, thus receiving the crown of popular acclamation. When we speak of a Casanova, we mean an irresistible champion, a devourer of women, a master seducer. In masculine mythology, the name is the counterpart of Helen, or

Phryne, or Ninon de Lenclos, in feminine. The son of a Venetian strolling player has received the unexpected honour of being incarnated as an amatory hero for all time. No doubt he has to share his pedestal with a companion, in this case a legendary figure. Beside him stands a man of bluer blood, obscurer nature, and more daimonic type—his Spanish rival, Don Juan. The latent contrast between these two masters in the art of seduction has often been pointed out, but the comparison, or rather the antithesis, has no more been exhausted than has the antithesis between Leonardo and Michelangelo, Tolstoy and Dostoyevsky, Plato and Aristotle.

The comparison between Casanova and Don Juan is reiterated generation after generation, each generation in turn being fascinated by the diversity-in-likeness of these two primal forms of eroticism. Although Casanova and Don Juan resemble one another in this respect, that they are both birds of prey, so far as women are concerned, continually pouncing on victims whose alarm is tinctured with delight, there is an essential distinction between the two types. As contrasted with Casanova, easygoing, unprincipled, free from inhibitions, Don Juan is restricted by the regulations of a caste; Don Juan is a *hidalgo*, a Spanish nobleman, and even in revolt he remains a Catholic by sentiment. As a Spaniard

pur sangre, in the depths of his heart, he is profoundly
influenced by the concept of honour; and as a medi-
aeval Catholic he unwittingly accepts the ecclesiastical
valuation of all carnality as "sin." From this tran-
scendental perspective of Christianity, extra-conjugal
love is satanic, is forbidden by God's ordinances, is a
heresy of the flesh—and is all the more alluring in
consequence! Casanova, the free-thinker, a child of
the Renaissance, laughs heartily at such antiquated
ideas. For Don Juan, woman is the instrument of
sin, and exists only to subserve the purposes of
"evil." Her very being is a seduction and a danger,
so that what seems to be the most perfect virtue in a
woman is but a semblance, and the trail of the ser-
pent is over it all. Don Juan does not believe in the
purity, the chastity, of any of this devil's brood; he
knows that under their clothes they are all equally
naked, all equally accessible to seduction. He is urged
on by an inner impulse to prove woman's fatal weakness by a thousand and one instances; to convince
himself, the world, and God that all these unapproachable *doñas*, these professedly faithful wives,
these ingenuous girls, these brides of Christ, are
without exception willing to admit the right sort of
wooer to their beds; he wants to prove that they are
only *anges à l'église et singes au lit*. Such a conviction,
such a determination, is what drives him onward

93

incessantly to renewed and reiterated acts of seduction.

Nothing, therefore, could be more misguided than to represent Don Juan, the arch-enemy of the female sex, as *amoroso*, as the universal lover of women, seeing that he is never moved by true love towards any of them. The elemental force that impels him against women is the primal hate that inspires the male. When he takes possession of a woman, he is not seizing that which he wishes to have for himself, but is taking away from her something he wishes to deprive her of, is despoiling her of her most precious treasure, her honour. His lust is not, like Casanova's, an affair of the seminal vesicles, but an affair of the brain. Spiritually, though not corporeally, he is a sadist, eager to degrade, to shame, to humiliate femininity at large. His enjoyment is reached by devious paths; it depends upon an imaginative anticipation of the despair the woman will feel when she has been possessed, dishonoured, disclosed in all her fleshliness. For Don Juan, therefore, the pleasures of the chase are intensified by its difficulties, in contrast with Casanova, who enjoys most the quarry which he finds easiest to run down. For the Spaniard, the more unapproachable a woman, and the more unlikely it seems that he will be able to win her, the greater and more convincing (as proof of his thesis) the ultimate triumph. Where there is no resistance, Don Juan finds no attraction. We cannot fancy him spending the night, like Casanova, with a harlot in a common brothel. His senses are only stimulated when he is engaged in the devilish work of debasing what he enjoys, of pushing his partner into sin, of leading her to commit a unique offence, one that can never be repeated, that of the first act of adultery, that of surrendering her virginity, or that of violating her sacred vow of chastity. As soon as he has had his will of such a woman, the experiment is finished, and the object of seduction has become a mere number in a register. He never wants to look caressingly again on the companion of last night, the one and only night. As little as the sportsman cares for the bird he has brought down, just so little does this professional seducer care about his victim once the experiment is over. He must go on with the hunt, must sacrifice the greatest possible number to his primal impulse, must continue for ever and a day to prove that all women are frail. Don Juan knows no rest, and in truth finds no enjoyment. He is the sworn enemy of woman, and the devil has equipped him with everything he needs for the campaign: wealth, youth, birth, bodily charm, and, most important of all, absolute callousness.

In actual fact a woman, as soon as she has been

defeated by his coldly calculating technique, regards Don Juan as the devil incarnate. All his victims hate today as ardently as they loved yesterday their arch-enemy, who on the morning after possession wounds them to the heart with his cold and scornful laughter. (Mozart has immortalized it.) They are ashamed of their weakness; they rail at the villain who has deceived them; and in his person they loathe the whole male sex. Doña Anna, Doña Elvira, and all the rest, having once yielded to his calculated impetuosity, remain thenceforward embittered, poisoned in spirit. The women, on the other hand, who have given themselves to Casanova, thank him as if he were a god, glad to remember his ardent embraces, for he has done nothing to wound their feelings, nothing to mortify them in their womanhood; he has bestowed upon them a new confidence in their own personality. The very thing which the Spanish satanist, Don Juan, forces them to despise as the depth of debasement, as bestial rut, as the most devilish of woman's weaknesses—the glowing ardours of the moment of surrender—Casanova, delicate master of the erotic art, persuades them to recognize as the true meaning, the holiest duty, of their feminine nature. Refusal, unwillingness to surrender, says this gentle priest and vigorous epicurean, is the sin against the holy ghost of the flesh, against the god-given significance of nature.

Thanks to his thankfulness, rapt by his raptures, they feel themselves freed from all blame and unloosed from every inhibition. With a caressing hand when he strips them of their clothing he strips them of all shyness and all anxiety—these half-women, who do not become wholly women until they have given themselves. He fills them with delight because he is himself delighted, he exculpates them for their enjoyment by his own grateful ecstasies. Casanova does not fully enjoy himself with a woman unless she shares his delight. "Four-fifths of my pleasure has always consisted in making women happy." For him, pleasure must be set off with pleasure, just as the lover demands love in return. His Herculean labours are undertaken to exhaust and delight not so much his own body as that of the woman he clasps in his arms.

Since he is thus an altruist in love, it would obviously be absurd for him to use force or artifice in order to secure the physical enjoyment he covets. Never, like Don Juan, does he desire crude possession; he must have a willing surrender. We have no right, therefore, to style him a seducer. He invites a woman to join him in a new and fascinating game, in which he would like the weary old world (burdened by inhibitions and scruples) to participate, finding a fresh impetus in Eros. Freedom from scruples, this and nothing else releases us from the chains which bind us to earth. Every woman who gives herself to him becomes more fully a woman, because she has grown more fully conscious, more pleasure-loving, freer from restraints. In her body, which she has hitherto regarded with indifference, she now discovers new and surprising sources of delight. For the first time, beneath the veil of shame she sees the beauty of her own femininity. A master spendthrift has taught her how to spend, how to give pleasure for pleasure, and not to ask for any meaning beyond that which she feels quickening in her senses. But it is not really he who has won the woman; her conquest has been effected by this joyfully accepted form of enjoyment. Hence new devotees of the faith become propagandists. A sister brings a sister to the altar, a mother hands her daughter over to this gentle teacher, every one of his mistresses invites others to join in the dance. Just as the sisterhood of women, in one of its manifestations, leads each of Don Juan's victims to warn (how vainly!) her sisters against the enemy of their sex, so does this same sense of sisterhood, in another of its manifestations, make the women who have been loved by Casanova proclaim him as the man who showers divine blessings on their sex. Just as he, when he loves a woman, loves in her woman as a whole, so do women love in him the symbol of the loving man and master.

As conqueror, then, Casanova is not a magician, not a wonder-worker in the realm of love. His powers of conquest are nature personified, they are nature's kindly powers; and the secret of his success is his amazing virility. Thoroughly natural in his desires, perfectly straightforward in his sensuality, he brings into love an admirable common sense, an accurate vital balance. He does not lift women to the level of saints, nor does he lower them to that of demons; he merely desires them on the earthly plane as companions in the game of love, as the God-given complements of male energy and desire. Although a more ardent being than all the lyric poets, he never exaggerates the idea of love to make of it the essential meaning of the world, for whose sake the stars circle round our little globe, for whose sake the seasons wax and wane, for whose sake mankind breathes and dies; never, like the pious Novalis, does he make of love the "Amen of the universe." With Hellenic frankness he looks upon Eros as nothing more and nothing less than the most entrancing enjoyment earth has to offer. Thus does Casanova bring love down out of imaginary heavens, down into the life of this world, where he can enjoy it in the person of every woman who has the courage and the will for joy. At the very time when Rousseau, the Frenchman, was discovering sentimentalism in love, and when Werther, the German, was discovering enthusiastic melancholy, Casanova, the Italian, was, by the impetus of his life, demonstrating the pagan cheerfulness of love to be the best helper in the ever necessary work of freeing the world from its burdens.

YEARS IN OBSCURITY

*How often in my life have I done something
which was repugnant to me, and which I
could not understand. But I was driven
onward by a secret power, which, wittingly,
I was unable to resist.*

CASANOVA, IN THE MEMOIRS

YOU HAVE NO RIGHT to blame women for surrendering so easily to the great seducer. Every
woman who encounters him falls into temptation,
and is ready to be enthralled by the fiery charm of
his art of life. Let us admit the fact that it is hard for
a man to read Casanova's memoirs without envy.
Who is there, engaged in routine occupations in this
fenced and specializing century of ours, who is not
seized from time to time by the spirit of adventure?
In such moments, our thoughts turn to the mad doings
of this arch-adventurer; his life filled full of snatch-
ings and enjoyments, his thorough-going epicure-
anism, seem to us wiser and more real than our own
orderly preoccupation with the things of the spirit;
his philosophy seems more vital than the peevish

doctrines of Schopenhauer or the cold dogmatism of Kant. What a poor thing at such moments appears our existence, safeguarded only by renunciation, when compared with his! It is with a sore heart that we recognize all we are paying for our spiritual poise and our life of moral endeavour—we are paying for it in restraints.

Such is our fate. Insofar as we try to look beyond the fleeting hour and to direct our endeavours towards some future aim, we deprive this present hour of some of its vitality; and insofar as we seek to transcend the present, we rob ourselves of present enjoyment. We look before and after, and the ball-and-chain of conscience clanks at our heels as we walk. We have surrendered ourselves as prisoners to our own selves, and that is why we are so heavy-footed. But Casanova is light-hearted and light-footed; he makes all women his own; he speeds across all lands; he drifts before the winds of chance through all the heavens and all the hells. No real man, therefore, I repeat, can read Casanova's memoirs in certain moods without feeling envious, without feeling himself to be a bungler as compared with this master of the art of life. Often—again and again and again—one would rather be Casanova than be Goethe, Michelangelo, or Balzac. Smile though we may, a little cynically, at the literary affectations and the *rodomontade* of this philosophically draped rascal, nevertheless in the sixth, the tenth, the twelfth volume we are often inclined to regard him as the wisest man in the world, and to look upon his philosophy of superficiality as the shrewdest and most entrancing of all doctrines.

Fortunately Casanova himself cures our prompting towards undue admiration. His register of the art of life has one serious flaw in it—he has forgotten old age. An epicurean technique of enjoyment, a technique entirely concerned with the sensual, the palpable, is exclusively based upon young and vigorous senses, upon the circulation of a young and vigorous bodily sap. As soon as the flame of life ceases to burn with youthful ardour, the whole philosophy of sensual pleasure will be found to have become an insipid, unpalatable broth. Only with tense muscles, with firm, white teeth, can we master life in Casanova's fashion. Woe to the epicurean when the muscles grow flaccid, when the teeth begin to fall out, when the senses lose their keenness; for then this agreeable, this comfortable philosophy will certainly be found to have lost its savour. In the man of pleasure (I use that term in its cruder sense), the curve of existence is inevitably a declining one. The spendthrift has no reserves, he squanders his substance in riotous living; while the man of the spirit, ostensibly practising renunciation, is really storing up an ample supply of energy in an accumulator. One who has devoted himself to the things of the spirit will, even in his declining years, and often (like Goethe) at a patriarchal age, be able to experience transformations, sublimations, purifications, and transfigurations. Though his blood has cooled, his life can still rise to dizzy heights of intellectual experience; and the bold play of his thoughts compensates him for the reduced intensity of bodily function. The man who has lived only for the pleasures of the senses, on the other hand, the man to whom nothing can appeal but corporeal impacts from without, sticks fast in old age like a waterwheel when the stream that should turn it has dried up. For him, to grow old is a decline into nullity instead of a transition to novelty. Life, an inexorable creditor, demands back from him with interest what his uncontrolled senses have spent too early and too quickly. Thus it is that Casanova's wisdom ends with his happiness, his happiness with his youth. He only seems wise as long as he is handsome, victorious, and in the full possession of his bodily energies. You may envy him until he is forty years of age, but you can only pity him for the rest of his life. Casanova's carnival, the most brightly coloured of any ever celebrated in Venice, ends prematurely and sadly upon a sombre Ash Wednesday.

We watch the shadows slowly creeping athwart his narrative, just as wrinkles form upon an ageing face. He has fewer and fewer triumphs to report, and more and more vexations to record. We find an ever more frequent mention of occurences (for which, of course, he is never to blame) in connection with spurious bills of exchange, false banknotes, pawned jewels; and we read less often of visits to princely courts. From London, he finds it necessary to steal away by night and in a fog, to escape the arrest that would have been inevitable a few hours later, and would have been a prelude to the gallows. From Warsaw, he is hunted away like a criminal. He is expelled both from Vienna and from Madrid. In Barcelona, he spends forty days under lock and key. Florence gives him notice to quit. In Paris, he receives a *lettre de cachet*, and has no choice but to leave the beloved city. Casanova is unwanted, is as unwelcome as a louse.

We are puzzled, at first, and ask ourselves what can be amiss that, of a sudden, the world should prove so ungracious to its former favorite, should talk so much about good morals. Has there been a change for the worse in his character, that people should cold-shoulder him in this way? No, he is the same as ever, is what he will be to the end of the chapter. He has always been a humbug. What is wrong with him is that he is beginning to lack self-confidence, the victorious self-confidence of youth. Where he has sinned most, there he finds his punishment. The women are the first to forsake their darling. A poor, pitiful little Delilah inflicts a terrible wound upon this Samson in the lists of love—(a crafty, good-for-nothing baggage, Charpillon by name, in London). This episode, the most effectively narrated of all in his memoirs, sketched with perfect artistry, is the turning-point. For the first time the experienced seducer is tricked by a woman, and not by a woman of standing, inaccessible, virtuous, and therefore refusing her favours, but by a spiteful little harlot, who makes him crazy with desire, strips him of his last coin, and refuses to allow him to lay so much as a finger upon her lecherous body. A Casanova who is contemptuously rejected though he pays and overpays; a Casanova despised, and compelled to look on while an impudent young fellow, a hairdresser's assistant, is made happy by the possession of all that he vainly covets and has paid for in hard coin—this is Casanova, wounded to the quick in his tenderest place, his vanity; and thenceforward he can never feel confident. Prematurely, when he is forty years of age, he is terrified to discover that the motor upon which his victorious progress through the world has depended is no longer working properly, and he becomes afraid that his progress will soon be arrested. "What troubled me most of all was that I must perforce admit the beginnings of that loss of power which is associated with the oncoming of age. I no longer had the careless confidence of youth." A Casanova without self-confidence, a Casanova without the overwhelming virility which has hitherto charmed women, lacking beauty and potency and money, no longer able to plume himself on being the darling both of Priapus and of Fortuna—what is he, now that he has lost this trump card?

Here is his own description: "A man of a certain age, to whom luck has become a stranger, and towards whom women have grown cold. A bird without wings, a man without virility, a lover without a mistress, a gambler without money to stake, a tired frame without tension or beauty." No longer does he sound triumphal peals, or proclaim the exclusive wisdom of enjoyment; for the first time the dangerous word "renunciation" finds expression in his philosophy. "The days when I made women in love with me are over; I must either renounce them, or else buy their favours." Renunciation, the most incredible thought for a Casanova, has become terribly real to him. He cannot buy women without money; yet it has always been women who have kept him in funds. The wonderful circulation has come to an end, the game is finished, and life has become a serious matter for the master of all adventurers. That is why the ageing Casanova, poor Casanova, from being a man of pleasure becomes a parasite, from being a man interested in the world for its own sake becomes a spy, from being a gambler becomes a cheat and a beggar; that is why the boon companion becomes a forlorn scribbler who is always quarrelling with his housemates.

A distressing spectacle! Casanova lays down his arms. The veteran of countless love battles grows cautious and modest. Quietly and sadly the great *commediante in fortuna* retires from the stage where he has had such splendid successes. He doffs his fine clothes as "no longer suitable to my position"; takes off his ring and his diamond shoebuckles, discarding therewith his glorious arrogance; throws his philosophy under the table like a worn pack of cards; bows his neck beneath the yoke, submitting himself to the law in virtue of which withered prostitutes become procuresses, gamblers become cardsharpers, adventurers become toadies. Now that the blood has ceased to course warmly through his veins, the sometime *citoyen du monde* begins to shiver, and to suffer from homesickness. Putting his pride in his pocket, repenting him of his offences, he begs the Venetian government for forgiveness. He writes lickspittle

reports to the inquisitors, composes a patriotic book-
let, a *refutatione* of the attacks on the Venetian government, in which he is not ashamed to declare that the
Leads, where he had pined in prison, are "a well-
ventilated place," an earthly paradise. Of these distressing episodes, there is no word in the memoirs,
which end prematurely, and tell the reader nothing
about the years of shame. He shrouds them in obscurity, lest he should blush; and we are inclined to congratulate ourselves for this, seeing that Casanova the
toady, Casanova the police spy, conflicts too painfully
with the doughty warrior of earlier days.

Thus for a few years there slinks across the *Merceria*
a corpulent and rubicund man, who is no longer
fashionably dressed. He listens attentively to all that
the Venetians are saying, sits in taverns watching
suspicious characters, and in the evenings writes
tedious reports to the inquisitors. They are signed
"Angelo Pratolini," the alias of a pardoned ex-con-
vict, who for a few gold pieces is willing to send others to the prison in which he himself had been confined in youth, the prison whose description has
made him famous. Casanova, Chevalier de Seingalt,
the darling of women, the victorious seducer, has
become Angelo Pratolini, informer and nark; the fingers that were once adorned with diamonds are now
busied in writing sordid denunciations, in sprinkling

ink and gall venomously to right and to left, until even Venice wearies of his complaints and expels him from its precincts.

Information is scanty as concerns Casanova's life during the next few years. Upon what gloomy seas did the wreck drift until it was at length cast ashore in Bohemia? The elderly adventurer still wandered to and fro across Europe, making trial of his customary arts in the hope of extracting money from the rich and the noble—cardsharper, cabalist, and pimp, as before. Alas, the favouring gods of his youth, his impudence, his self-confidence, had abandoned him; women laughed at his wrinkled face, and he was hard put to it to get a living. He became secretary (probably a euphemism for spy) at the embassy in Vienna; and there is evidence of expulsion from a number of towns. In Vienna, at long last, he designed to marry a streetwalker, that the earnings of her sorry but lucrative trade might provide him with the wherewithal to live; this excellent scheme came to nothing. At length Count Waldstein, a man fabulously rich, with a taste for the occult, came across Casanova in Paris, and took pity on him, charmed by the derelict's cynical volubility. He invited the adventurer to Dux as librarian, which meant court jester. Waldstein bought Casanova as he would have bought any other curio, paying for this one a thousand gulden a year—a salary which was always pledged in advance to Casanova's creditors. At Dux the old man lived, or rather died, for thirteen years.

After a long period of obscurity, he once more becomes plainly visible. He is Casanova again, or at any rate something which vaguely reminds us of Casanova. He is Casanova's mummy, a withered vestige, pickled in his own gall, a strange specimen which the count shows to guests. They look upon him as an extinct crater, entertaining, no longer dangerous, lively and amusing after the southland fashion, but slowly perishing of boredom in this Bohemian eyrie. Yet for the last time Casanova fools the world. While all think him utterly outworn, dead to life and a candidate for the cemetery, he makes a new life for himself out of his memories, and, in a supreme venture, ensures for himself immortality.

LIKENESS OF CASANOVA
IN OLD AGE

Altera nunc rerum facies, me quaero, nec adsum. Non sum,
qui fueram, non putor esse: fui.

INSCRIPTION BENEATH CASANOVA'S PORTRAIT
AT THE AGE OF SIXTY-THREE

WE ARE IN the years 1797 and 1798. The
bloodstained *besom* of the revolution has been
sweeping up the debris of the gallant century; the
heads of His Most Christian Majesty and of Queen
Marie Antoinette have fallen into the basket of the
guillotine; and now a little general from Corsica has
made short work of dozens of petty princes, the
Venetian inquisitors not excepted. Nobody is reading
the *Encyclopædia* any longer, or the writings of Voltaire
and Rousseau, for interest is concentrated upon the
bulletins from the seat of war. Europe is a sober place;
carnival days are over, and with them have vanished
rococo, hooped petticoats, powdered wigs, silver shoebuckles, and Brussels lace. Velvet coats are out of
fashion; everyone who is not in uniform wears plain
cloth. But here is a strange figure, an old fellow

113

rusticating in an out-of-the-way corner of Bohemia, who seems to have taken no note of the passing of time. Like Herr Ritter Gluck in Hoffman's tale, he is decked out in all the colours of the rainbow, velvet waistcoat with gold buttons, neckcloth of worn and yellow lace, clocked stockings, flowered garters, and white-plumed hat. In this rig, he leaves Castle Dux and makes his way over the cobblestones into the town. He still wears a wig, carelessly, powdered it is true (for he no longer has a servant), and he leans on a goldheaded cane such as might have been seen in the Palais Royal more than half a century before. Yes, it is really Casanova, or rather his mummy; he is still alive, despite poverty, manifold vexations, and syphilis. His skin is like parchment; his great hooked nose projects formidably over his thin-lipped, slavering mouth; his bushy brows are white; he exhales a stuffy aroma, as of dried gall and book-dust. But his eyes, black as pitch, have the old restless gleam, peering angrily from beneath the half-closed lids. Their expression is not a pleasant one, for he has been a peevish fellow ever since fortune cast him on to this Bohemian dung-hill. He vouchsafes scarcely a glance at the stupid townsfolk; they are hardly worth a civil greeting, these clownish fellows who have never been outside their native village. "What is there in common between them and myself, the Chevalier de Seingalt, who once fired a bullet into the august body of the court chamberlain of Poland, and who received the golden spurs from the pope's own hands?" Sad to relate, even the women do not respect him. They hold their hands in front of their mouths, to keep themselves from laughing at him openly. Still, it is better to walk abroad among these common folk than to sit at home among those blackguards of servants, "the blockheads whose kicks I have to endure"; Feltkirchner worst of all, the steward, and Widerholt, his tool. What brutes they are! On purpose, yesterday, they emptied the saltcellar into the soup, and burned the macaroni; they tore his portrait out of his *Icosameron*, and hung it up in the privy; they actually dared to whip the little bitch Melampyge which countess Roggendorf had given him, simply because the poor beast had misbehaved in one of the rooms. Oh for the good old days when one would have put such unruly servants in the stocks, or have been able to order them a sound flogging, instead of having to endure their insolence. But today, thanks to Robespierre, the *canaille* has the upper hand, the Jacobins have ruined everything, and he himself is nothing more than a poor old dog whose teeth are worn out. Well, well, what's the use of grumbling; he had better go back to his room and read Horace.

Today his troubles are forgotten for the moment,

and the old mummy is bustling about in fine fettle. He has put on his threadbare court dress, and is wearing all his orders, for the count has personally informed him that his grace of Teplitz is coming, accompanied by the Prince de Ligne and other noblemen. They will talk French at table, and the envious pack of servants will have to stand behind his chair and treat him as one of the distinguished company, to hand him his food properly, instead of throwing it to him as one throws a bone to a dog. Yes, he will sit down to dinner at the big table among the Austrian noblemen, who know how to value sprightly conversation, how to listen to a philosopher whom even Voltaire respected, one who in former days was a welcome guest at the table of emperors and kings. Perhaps after the ladies have withdrawn, Count Waldstein and the Prince de Ligne will ask him to read a chapter from his interesting memoirs. He will probably comply—probably, not certainly, for he is not Count Waldstein's servant, and compelled to obey orders; he is a guest, a librarian, an equal. Anyhow, he will tell them one or two good stories, in the style of his sometime teacher, Monsieur Crébillon; or one or two spicy tales of the Venetian sort. "We shall all be noblemen together, and shall understand the finer shades. We shall laugh merrily over our wine, a dark and heavy burgundy like that drunk at the court of

His Most Christian Majesty; shall converse about war, alchemy, and books; and an elderly philosopher will certainly be able to impart a little of his wisdom concerning the world and women."

Greatly excited, he hobbles through the suite of rooms, looking like a withered and malicious bird, his eyes sparkling with arrogance and spite. He polishes up the false gems in the cross he is going to wear (the genuine stones have gone to the Jews long since); standing in front of the mirror, he practises bowing after the manner of the court of Louis XV. It is a pity that he has grown stiff, that his back creaks when he tries to bend it, but what can you expect when one has been driving in *postchaises* over the length and breadth of Europe for seventy years, and when the women have drained away one's sap? Still, the wits have not all run out of his brain; he will know how to make a good showing and to amuse the company. In the best handwriting he can achieve—it is rather tremulous, but still beautifully legible—he copies out on a piece of handmade paper a poem in the French tongue, a poem of welcome to the Princesse de Recke; and he paints a pompous dedication on the front of his new comedy for the amateur stage. Even while vegetating here in Dux, he has not forgotten the proprieties, and, as a gentleman, he knows how to greet an assembly of persons interested in literature.

Nor is he disappointed when the carriages drive up to the door, and, on his gouty feet, he stumps down the steps to welcome the newcomers. While Count Waldstein and the guests toss their headgear and their cloaks to the servants, they embrace Casanova as a member of their own order, and to those who have not met him before he is presented as the famous Chevalier de Seingalt. There is talk of his literary merits, and the ladies vie with one another to have him sitting beside them at table. Even before the dishes have been cleared away, everything happens as he had foreseen. The Prince de Ligne asks how he is getting on with that extraordinarily interesting account of his life; and thereupon, with one voice, the ladies and gentlemen beg him to read them a chapter from the book. How can he refuse to comply with any wish of his benefactor, Count Waldstein? Casanova trots upstairs to his room, and from among the fifteen manuscript folios he selects the volume in which the marker lies. This contains the show piece, one of the few chapters it is safe to read in mixed company, the account of his escape from the Leads in Venice. He has related this incomparable adventure so often: to the Elector of Bavaria, to the Elector of Cologne, to men of high rank in England and in Poland. He will show them that a Casanova can write more spiritedly than that heavy Prussian Herr von Trenck, about whose escape from prison so much fuss has been made. Recently Casanova has introduced some fine new turns of phrase, has dwelt upon some remarkable complications, and has finished up with a most effective quotation from the divine Dante. The reading is a great success. There are salvos of applause; the count embraces him, and as he does so slips a rouleau of ducats into the old fellow's pocket. Well, Casanova can find a use for them. Though the world in general may have forgotten him, his creditors are well informed as to his whereabouts! But he is sincerely touched by these attentions, and the tears actually course down his cheeks when the princess congratulates him in kindly words, and when all drink to the speedy completion of his masterpiece.

Next day, alas, the horses have been put to and are pawing the ground impatiently in the courtyard. The noble company is about to start for Prague, and, although the librarian has hinted more than once that he has urgent business in that city, no one offers him a lift. He must stay behind in the huge, cold, draughty castle, exposed to the insolence of the rabble of servants, who are ready to grin contemptuously at Casanova the instant Count Waldstein's back is turned. He is left alone among barbarians, not one of whom can speak French or Italian, not one of whom can converse about Ariosto and Jean-Jacques. He cannot spend all his time writing letters to the dry-as-dust Herr Opitz, in Czaslau, and to the small number of good-natured ladies who still keep up a correspondence with him. The spirit of boredom has once more taken possession of these uninhabited rooms, and the gout, which he had managed to forget yesterday, has returned in full force today. Grumpily Casanova takes off his court dress, and dons his thick Turkish dressing-gown; splenetically he sidles off to his last refuge, to his memories, to his writing-table. Carefully mended quills are waiting for him beside the blank folios on which he is to write. He sets himself to his task once more, and posterity may bless the tedium which induces him to write the story of his life.

For behind this death's-head countenance, behind this parchmenty skin, a vigorous memory has been preserved in excellent condition, like the flesh of a nut inside a hard and wrinkled shell. All remains in good order within the brain betwixt forehead and occiput. The sparkling eyes, the eager nostrils, the clutching hands, the gouty fingers—his memory retains all that they have seen, all that they have handled, in a thousand adventures; can recall every detail of the smooth feminine bodies which the fingers had once so ardently caressed. Now the fingers set themselves to writing of these things for thirteen hours at a stretch ("thirteen hours which pass in a flash as if they had been thirteen minutes"). Lying on the table is a medley of the faded letters from his sometime mistresses, mementos, locks of hair, all kinds of relics; and just as a silvery smoke will still rise above the embers when the flames are quenched, so an invisible cloud of delicate aroma hovers over the ancient momentos. Every embrace, every kiss, every surrender, is called up to play its part in the phantasmagoria; and this conjuration of the past is not work but play, *Le plaisir de se souvenir ces plaisirs.* The old man's eyes shine brightly; his lips twitch in his excitement; he mutters to himself as he reshapes dialogues, involuntarily mimicking his inamoratas' voices, and laughing as he retells his own jests. He forgets to eat and to drink; forgets his poverty, his lowly situation, and his impotence; forgets the sorrows and ignominies of his old age. In this dream life, he has grown young once again; Henriette, Babette, and Thérèse, the shades he has summoned from the dead, are smiling on him again, and perhaps he enjoys their necromantic presence even more than he enjoyed them in the flesh. He writes and writes, an adventurer with the pen as aforetime he was an adventurer with his whole ardent body; he paces up and down the room, reading over to himself what he has written, laughing heartily, self-forgetful. His enemies the servants have gathered round the door, wonderingly, eavesdropping. They grin at one another, and say: "To whom is he chattering, with whom is he laughing, the old fool?" Tapping their foreheads significantly, they clatter downstairs again to their wine, and leave Casanova to himself in his garret. The outer world has forgotten him. The angry old eagle, alone in his eyrie at Dux, might almost as well be living on the top of an iceberg. When at length, at the end of June, 1798, his tired heart has ceased to beat, and the poor, withered frame which had once been so ardently embraced by a thousand women is committed to the tomb, the church register cannot even get his name right. "Casaneus, Venetian, eighty-four years of age," is the entry; wrong name, wrong age, so little do those among whom he has lived for years, and among whom he has now died, know of him. No one troubles to erect a monument, and no one pays any heed to his manuscripts. While the body moulders in an unnamed grave, the letters crumble, and even thievish hands are not interested enough to open or to steal the folio volumes of his memoirs. From 1798 to 1822 for a quarter of a century, no one could have seemed more hopelessly dead than this most living of all the men that ever lived.

GENIUS FOR
SELF-PORTRAITURE

Courage is the one thing needful.
PREFACE TO THE MEMOIRS

HIS LIFE had been adventurous, and his resurrection was to be the same. On December 13th, 1820 (who, at that date, remembered Casanova?) the famous publishing firm of Brockhaus received a letter from an unknown correspondent named Gentzel, inquiring whether the *Histoire de ma vie jusqu'à l'an 1797* by a certain Signor Casanova would be acceptable for publication. Brockhaus asked Gentzel to send along the folios, and secured an expert opinion on them. You may imagine that they created a sensation. The manuscript was instantly purchased, was translated into German, abominably mutilated one may presume, plastered over with fig-leaves, and adjusted for public consumption. By the time the fourth volume appeared, the success had been so tremendous that a Parisian pirate retranslated the German translation into French, the work being thus mauled a second time. Thereupon Brockhaus, with an eye to his own profits, shot a second French retranslation after the first. In a word, Giacomo, the rejuvenated, had come to life again. He now enjoys a vigorous rein-carnation in all the towns he ever visited—but his original manuscript is solemnly entombed in Herr Brockhaus' safe, and only God and Brockhaus know through what devious and thievish paths the volumes wandered during their three-and-twenty years of incognito, or how much of their precious contents has been lost, mutilated, castrated, falsified. In the genuine Casanova style, the whole affair reeks of mystery, adventure, dishonesty. Still, all these draw-backs notwithstanding, we can congratulate our-selves on the miracle of possessing the most impu-dent and racy picaresque romance of all ages.

Casanova himself had never seriously believed in the public appearance of this monster. "For seven years I have been doing nothing else than write my memoirs," confesses the gouty old hermit on one occasion, "and it has gradually become a necessity for me to carry the matter through to an end, although I greatly regret having undertaken it. But I write in the hope that my history will never see the light of day. Apart from the fact that the censorship, that extinguisher of the intellect, would never allow it to be printed, I look forward to being rational enough in my last illness to have all the manuscript burnt before my eyes." Fortunately he remained true to himself, and therefore never became "rational." What he once spoke of as his capacity for "secondary blushing," for blushing at his inability to blush, did not prevent his taking up his pen, and, in his fair, round hand, writing folio after folio for twelve hours a day. He said of this occupation: "It was the only way in which I could hinder myself from becoming crazy, or from dying of the spleen of vexation on account of the privations and annoyances I had to suffer daily at the hands of the envious brutes who lived under the same roof with me in Count Waldstein's castle."

As fly-flapper to ward off boredom, a remedy against intellectual ossification—surely this is a strange motive, the objector will exclaim, for the writing of one's memoirs. But it would be a mistake to underrate the importance of tedium as an incentive to literary creation. We have to thank the weary years spent in prison by Cervantes for the boon of Don Quixote; the best pages written by Stendhal were penned during his exile in the marshes of Civita Vecchia; even Dante's *Divine Comedy* might never have come into being but for the author's banishment, for had he stayed in Florence he would have written in blood with sword and battleaxe instead of committing his thoughts to rhyme. The most brightly coloured pictures of life can only be fashioned in a *camera obscura*. Had Count Waldstein taken the worthy Giacomo with him to Paris or to Vienna, fed him there on the fat of the land and allowed him to smell the flesh of women, had he been fêted as a wit in all the drawing-rooms, these wonderful narratives would never have got beyond the stage of talk over chocolate and sherbet, would never have achieved permanent incorporation in black and white. Like Ovid beside the shores of the Euxine, the old fellow sat alone and shivering in his Bohemian exile, and there told his story like one looking back on life out of the realm of the shades. His friends were dead, his adventures had been forgotten, his senses had ceased to glow. A neglected ghost, he wandered through the chilly rooms of the castle. No woman came to visit him; no one had any respect for him; no one wanted to hear him talk. The venerable sorcerer, therefore, wishing to prove, to himself at least, that he was still alive, or at any rate had lived (*vixi, ergo sum*), exerted his cabalistic arts once more to conjure up the past, recounted for his present enjoyment the enjoyments of days long dead. Hungry men lacking money to buy food must feast upon the odour of roast meat; victims on the field of war and the field of Venus must content themselves as best they may with telling the story of their adventures. "I renew the pleasure by reminding myself of it, and I can laugh at past distresses since I can no longer feel their smart."

Casanova's sole purpose in operating this peep-show, this old man's toy, is to please himself; he wants his vivid memories to distract his attention from the dull present. It is this negative element of absolute aloofness and unconcern which gives his work its peculiar psychological value as self-portraiture. Generally speaking, when anyone tells the story of his own life, he does it purposively, and somewhat theatrically. He puts himself on a stage, is aware of the audience, unconsciously adopts some particular attitude, poses as an interesting character, calculates the effects of every gesture. Benjamin Franklin writes his autobiography as a work of edification; Bismarck, as a historical document; Jean-Jacques Rousseau, to make a sensation; Goethe, as a work of art and an imaginative exercise; Napoleon on St Helena, as a justification and as a monument. They all expect the work of self-portraiture to have a specific influence in the moral, historical, or literary field and for every one of them this conviction imposes a burden or exercises a restraint in the form of a sense of respon-sibility. Famous men are never free from fears and scruples when writing autobiography, for they know that their self-portrait will be confronted with a portrait that already exists in the imaginations or experiences of countless fellow-men. Willy-nilly, therefore, they are compelled to adapt the autobiography to the preconceived legend. Being famous, for the sake of their fame they are constrained to have regard for their country, their children, morality, honour. Instinctively they watch the image of their personality that has shaped itself in the minds of their contemporaries; and one who already belongs to the public is bound by many ties.

Casanova, on the other hand, can enjoy the luxury of absolute freedom from restrictions, and can indulge in the impudence of anonymity. He is under obligations to no one, has no ties, either to the past, which has forgotten him, or to the future, in which he does not believe. He is not troubled by any considerations for family feeling, by any thought of morality, by any circumstantial hindrances. His children, if he has any, have been hatched out of cuckoos' eggs laid in strange nests. The women who gave themselves to him in the days of his youth have been mouldering long since in Italian, Spanish, English, or German earth. He has no fatherland, no home, no religion. Whose feelings need he consider? What he has to tell can no longer advantage him in any way; nor can it harm him, since for practical purposes he is a dead man, is beyond good and evil beyond respect and contempt, beyond approval and disapproval, expunged from men's memories, a dead star, or one which glows only in its hidden core. "Why should I not tell the truth? A man cannot deceive himself, and I am writing for myself alone."

But when Casanova speaks of telling the truth, he does not imply a determination to drive mine-shafts into his own interior, to disclose psychological depths. He means no more than that he will have no inhibitions, no shame. He will strip off his clothes, and, comfortably naked, will warm his body once again in the stream of sensuality, will splash cheerfully in the current of memories, taking no heed of the presence of actual or imaginary spectators. He does not recount his adventures like a literary man, a soldier, or a poet, like one who talks for his own honour and glory; he writes in the spirit in which a bravo vaunts the murders he has committed, or a poor old harlot tells of her hours of love—with no thought of shame. *Non erubesco evangelium*, I do not blush at my confessions, such is the motto written underneath his *Précis de ma vie*, the first draft of his memoirs. He tells his story simply and directly. Thus while he may seem coarse at times, writing as frankly as Lucian, and (like a vain athlete showing off his muscle) making too public a display of his phallic activities—assuredly this shameless parade is far more to our taste than the cowardly furtiveness of a weak-loined *galanterie in eroticis*. Look, for contrast, at the other erotic treatises of his day; at the rose-tinted, musk-smelling frivolities of a Grécourt, a Crébillon, or at Louvet de Couvray's *Faublas*, in which Eros is draped as a shepherd-boy and love is displayed as a lascivious *chassé-croisé*, a gallant amusement, in which one neither procreates children nor catches syphilis. In Casanova's memoirs we have nothing of this sort; we have precise descriptions of the wholesome and exuberant joys of a vigorous man of the senses, whose elemental virility and elemental naturalness we can fully appreciate. In Casanova, masculine love is not depicted as a delicate, gently flowing rivulet in which sportive nymphs can cool their feet; but as a mighty river, reflecting the world in its surface, and at the same time sweeping along in its depths all the slime and foulness of existence. Assuredly no other autobiographer can rival him in his illumination of the Pan-like intensity of the male sexual impulse. At length we find someone with courage enough to disclose the intermingling of flesh and spirit in masculine love; with courage enough to describe, not only sentimental *amourettes*, but also the adventures of the brothel, stark-naked and skin-deep sexuality; the whole labyrinth of sex, through which every real man threads his way.

Not that the other great autobiographies, like those of Goethe or Rousseau, are positively unveracious. But there is a falsehood that finds expression in telling only half the tale, and there is a falsehood that takes the form of concealment. Now both Goethe and Rousseau (like all autobiographers, with the possible exception of the bold Hans Jaeger) are careful (deliberately or forgetfully) to avoid saying a word about the less appetizing, the purely sexual episodes of their amatory life. They dwell exclusively upon spiritualized, sentimentalized love affairs with Claras and Gretchens. They tell us only of those women who, mentally as well as physically, are reasonably clean, are persons with whom they would not be ashamed to walk arm-in-arm down Main Street. The other women with whom our autobiographers have had carnal relations are kept carefully out of the way in dark alleys and in hidden terraced houses. Thus, unconsciously of course, these writers falsify the picture of masculine eroticism. Goethe, Tolstoy, even Stendhal who in other respects is no prude, having uneasy consciences, skate swiftly over the thin ice. They tell us nothing of their numerous encounters with *Venus Vulgivaga*, the earthly, all-too-earthly love. Were it not for the splendidly shameless Casanova, who boldly draws back all the curtains and lets us look freely into his inner rooms, world

131

literature would lack a thoroughly plain and straight-forward account of the complexities of masculine sexuality. In Casanova we are shown the whole sexual mechanism of the senses at work; we are shown the world of the flesh even in its miry and marshy parts; we are allowed to glimpse its abysses. This idler, adventurer, cardsharper, rogue, shows more straight-forwardness than the greatest of our writers, for he presents the world as a conglomerate of beauty and ugliness, of refined spirit and gross sexuality; and he does not pretend that it is nothing more than an ide-alized, chemically purified entity. In sexual matters, Casanova does not merely tell the truth, but (how immense is the difference) the whole truth. His love world is true to reality.

Casanova true? I hear the academicians stirring indignantly in their chairs. For the last fifty years they have been directing a machine-gun fire at his histor-ical blunders, and they have caught him out in many an outrageous falsehood. Gently, brothers, gently! No doubt Casanova was an accomplished cardsharper, was a habitual liar, was a professor of *rodomontade*. In his memoirs he arranges his cards here and there, *il corrige la fortune*, being an irreclaimable swindler, with a taste for giving lame chance a leg-up. He adorns, garnishes, peppers, spices his aphrodisiac ragout, mingling therein all the ingredients of an imagination

inflamed by abstinence. Often he does this automat-
ically, without being aware of it. We must remember
that in course of time, embellishments and even falsehoods are justified by memory, so that in the end a
genuine fabulist can no longer be certain what parts
of his story are fact and what fiction. Casanova, be it
remembered, was a rhapsodist. He paid for his invi-
tations to dine at great men's tables by being a good
conversationalist, by recounting strange adventures.
Just as court singers of old intensified interest by
interweaving new and ever new episodes into their
lays, so was he constrained to put a fresh romantic
gloss upon successive recitals of his adventures. For
instance, every time he had to retell the story of his
escape from the Leads it was expedient to heighten
the interest by a further exaggeration of the risks,
and he thus continually found himself at a greater
remove from the actual facts. He, poor fellow, could
never have anticipated that more than a century
after his death the members of a sort of historical
Casanova Police Force would be busily engaged in
combing through a mass of documents, letters, arch-
ives, in order to check every detail in his memoirs,
and in order, with the ruler of science, to rap him
on the knuckles for every mistake in a date.

No doubt his dates are not altogether reliable. As
for his anecdotes, quite a number of them, when

closely examined, collapse like a house of cards. For instance, it has been proved today, almost beyond doubt, that the romantic adventures in Constantinople were nothing more than a voluptuous dream of the old gentleman at Dux, and that he had quite gratuitously introduced poor Cardinal de Bernis as lover and voyeur into the story of his liaison with the pretty nun M. M. He reports meetings in Paris and London with persons who are positively known to have been elsewhere at the time; he gives a date ten years too early for the death of the Marchioness of Urfé, because her presence on the stage had become inconvenient to him; in a single hour, when plunged in thought, he walks from Zurich to Kloster Einsiedeln—thus covering a distance of thirty-one kilometres with the speed of a modern motor-car. Certainly you must not expect to find in him a fanatical zeal for truth in matters of detail, you must not consult him as a trustworthy historian. The more we scrutinize Casanova's statements in these little matters, the more frequent and the more flagrant are the minor errors we discover. But all these petty falsifications, chronological mistakes, mystifications, and vapourings, these arbitrary and often extremely natural errors of omission, count for nothing as compared with the uncompromising and positively unique veracity of the autobiography as a whole. No doubt Casanova has made free use of the artist's incontestable right to compress space and time in order to make incidents more picturesquely intelligible; but nothing of this sort affects the straightforward, frank, and luminous way in which he contemplates his life and his epoch as a whole. It is not Casanova alone, but the century to which he belongs, that are staged vividly before us. In dramatic episodes, electrifying in their contrasts, he exhibits all strata of society, of nations, of scenes, and paints for us a picture of eighteenth century morals and immorals unrivalled in literature.

At first sight you may regard it as a defect that he does not plumb the depths; and that he does not, like Stendhal or Goethe, view things from a height whence he can secure a general intellectual view of national peculiarities. But for the very reason that his outlook is a superficial one, that he stands within the bounds of the events he describes, looking inquisitively to right and to left of him, his method of contemplation makes his account so valuable a document to the historian of civilization.

Certainly, Casanova does not disclose the conceptual roots of the life amid which he lives, and is therefore unable to explain the totality of the phenomena he describes. He is content to leave everything as he finds it, higgledy-piggledy, the sport of chance, without any

attempt to assort, to crystallize. For him everything
is equally important, so long as it amuses him—that
was the only standard by which he and his associ-
ates judged. He knows neither large nor small in the
world of thought or in the world of things; has no
knowledge of good and evil. That is why he
describes his conversation with Frederick the Great
in exactly the same tone, and with exactly the same
amount of detail, as, ten pages earlier, he has
described a conversation with a harlot; that is why
he has, and expects you to have, just as much interest in a Paris brothel as in Empress Catherine's
Winter Palace. How many hundred ducats he has
won at faro, or how many times in a single night
he was able to prove his virility with Dubois or with
Hélène, is no less momentous to Casanova than are
the details of his talk with Monsieur de Voltaire.
For him nothing in the world has any moral or
æsthetic significance, and therefore he remains perfectly natural, perfectly at his ease, whatever he is
telling us. If Casanova's memoirs, intellectually con-
sidered, may seem no more than a commonplace
story of travel through the interesting landscapes of
life, this is as much as to say that there is no philosophy in them; but their very lack in this respect has
made of them a historical Baedeker, an eighteenth
century *Cortigiano*, and an amusing *chronique scandaleuse*,

a most effective cross-section from the everyday life of a century.

It is thanks to Casanova, in large measure, that we know so much of the daily life of the eighteenth century; of its balls, its theatres, coffee houses, festivals, inns, dining halls, brothels, hunting parties, monasteries, nunneries, and fortresses. Thanks to him we know how people travelled, fed, gamed, danced, lived, loved, amused themselves; we know their manners and customs, their ways of speech. Added to this abundance of facts, to this wealth of practical details, we have a tumultuous assembly of human personalities, enough to fill twenty novels and to supply ten generations of novelists. Look at them: soldiers and princes, popes and kings, cheats and card-sharpers, merchants and lawyers, castrati, *souteneurs*, women of all sorts and stations, authors and philosophers, the wise and the foolish—assuredly it is the best-stocked menagerie of human beings that any one writer has ever packed into the enclosure of a single book. None the less, each of the figures on his canvas has an unexplored interior. Casanova once said, writing to Opitz, that he lacked a talent for psychology, that he could not "discern inner physiognomies." We need not be surprised, therefore, that countless imaginative writers of later generations have drawn their must from this southland vineyard.

Hundreds of novels and plays owe to Casanova their
best characters and their most likely situations. Nor
is the quarry exhausted. Just as ten generations have
taken from the Forum stone for new buildings, so for
generations yet to come will writers borrow material
from this arch-spendthrift.

But the supreme character in his book—never to
be forgotten, and already within a century become
proverbial—is Casanova himself, that strange cross
between Renaissance adventurer and modern gallant, that amazing creature who was rascal and
genius rolled into one. People will never cease to
take delight in the study of his personality. As chal-
lengingly erect as the bronze equestrian statue of his
fellow-Venetian Colleoni, he stands sturdily planted
in the midst of life, looking down through the centuries, indifferent to mockery or blame. Shamelessly
he has displayed himself to the world, so that we
know better than we know our own brothers this
titanic, unwearied fragment of mankind. We should
waste our time were we to look for psychological
depths, to seek backgrounds and hidden abysses;
Casanova has nothing of the kind to reveal. There is
no rouge on his face, and he is unbuttoned down to
the codpiece of his breeches. Without ceremony, without restraint, without ambiguity he takes the reader
comfortably by the arm, reveals all his privacies,

whether of bed or board, whether of gaming table or alchemist's hocus-pocus. He laughingly displays himself in the most delicate situations, and he does so, not in an exhibitionist spirit, not under stress of a morbid Candaules perversion, but naïvely, with the inborn and bewitching grace of a child of nature, who has been in paradise, has seen there the naked Eve, and has not eaten of the apple which brings a knowledge of good and evil.

Here, as always, simplicity, ingenuousness, explains the perfection with which he tells his tale. The most skilful psychologist, the most practised writer, cannot make of Casanova a more live figure than he makes of himself in virtue of his absolute, unreflecting nonchalance. He stands before our eyes in all sorts of situations. We see him in anger, when his face flushes, when his white teeth are clenched, when his mouth is bitter as gall; we see him in danger, bold, alert, smiling contemptuously, with a steady hand on the hilt of his sword. We see him in good society; vain, boastful, self-possessed, talking easily, voluptuously appraising the charms of women. Whether as a handsome stripling or as a toothless ruin, he is always vividly presented to us. When we read his memoirs, we feel as if he were actually before us; and we are sure that if this man, dead long since, were to come suddenly round the corner, we should recognize him in a moment— though we know him only through a self-portrait illuminated by one who was neither a professional author nor a psychologist. Goethe's Werther, Kleist's Kohlhaas, Jean-Jacques Rousseau's Saint-Preux and Héloïse—not one of the figures made real to us by these great writers is so real as the self-portrayed Casanova.

It is of no use, therefore, to turn up your nose at his equivocal talent, or to put on moral airs because of his scapegrace behaviour, or to hold him to account for his banalities and ignorant plagiarisms in matters philosophical. Despite all you can do, despite all the objections you can raise, Giacomo Casanova has taken his place in world literature, beside the gallows-bird Villon, and various other rogues, who will outlive countless thoroughly reputable authors and critics. As when he was alive, so after his death, he has reduced to absurdity all the accepted laws of æsthetics, and has thrown the moral catechism into the wastepaper basket. The growth and the persistence of his reputation show that a man need not be especially gifted, industrious, well-behaved, noble-minded, and sublime, in order to make his way into the temple of literary immortality. Casanova has proved that one may write the most amusing story in the world without being a novelist, and may give the most admirable picture of the time without being a

historian; for in the last resort we judge these matters, not by the method but by the effect, not by the
morality but by the power. Any thoroughly adequate
feeling may be productive, shamelessness just as
much as shame, characterlessness just as much as
character, evil just as much as good, morality just as
much as immorality. What decides whether a man
will become immortal, is not his character but his
vitality. Nothing save intensity confers immortality.
A man manifests himself more vividly, in proportion
as he is strong and unified, effective and unique.
Immortality knows nothing of morality or immorality,
of good or evil; it measures only work and strength; it
demands from a man not purity but unity. Here,
morality is nothing; intensity, all.

AFTERWORD

The proper study of mankind is man.
ALEXANDER POPE

IN THE SERIES of volumes whose general title is *Master Builders**, I am trying to analyze the distinctive types of the creative will, and to illustrate these various types by a description of personalities characteristic of each. For the adept in self-portraiture, the aim is to disclose the microcosm of his own ego, rather than to depict the macrocosm, the plenitude of existence. Unconscious though it be, this is the purpose of his art; no reality is so important to him as the reality of his own life. Whereas the imaginative writer who creates new worlds beside the real world of objective experience, a writer whose gaze is fixed on the outer world, the extrovert, merges his

* *Casanova* originally formed part of the volume by Stefan Zweig entitled *Adepts in Self-Portraiture* which covered Tolstoy, Stendhal, and Casanova; this was part of a larger series entitled Master Builders which included Dickens, Balzac and Dostoyevsky. The final section, *The Struggle with the Daimon*, included Hölderlin, Kleist and Nietzsche.

ego so thoroughly in the objective that the ego is no longer discernible (Shakespeare is the supreme example)—the writer whose gaze is turned inward, the introvert, makes everything in the real world lead back into his own personality, so that his writings tend before all to be expositions of his own ego. No matter what form he may choose, the drama, the epic poem, lyric verse, or autobiography, he will unawares make his own self the medium and the centre of all his works, so that every one of them will primarily be an example of self-portraiture.

Casanova is the lowest, the primitive gradation of self-portraiture as a creative function. In him we have naïve self-portraiture, a simple record of deeds and happenings, without any attempt to appraise them, or to study the deeper working of the self.

At first glance it might seem as if self-portraiture would be an artist's most spontaneous and easiest task. Whom does the imaginative writer know better than himself? Here is a personality whose every experience is familiar, whose secrets have all been revealed, whose most intimate chambers have been unlocked. With no further trouble than a probing of memory and a description of the facts of life, he will reveal "the truth." He will have little more to do than to raise the curtain which hides the stage from the public. Just as no gifts for painting are requisite for photography, the unimaginative and purely mechanical reproduction of a prearranged reality, so, it would seem, the art of self-portraiture does not need an artist at all, but only an accurate registrar. On that theory, anyone you please could be a successful autobiographer.

The history of literature shows, however, that ordinary autobiographers are nothing better than commonplace witnesses testifying to facts which chance has brought to their knowledge. A practised artist, one with eyes to see, is needed to discern the innermost happenings of the soul; few even of the accomplished artists that have attempted autobiography have been successful in the performance of this difficult and responsible task. The path by which a man must descend from the surface into the depths, from the breathing present into the overgrown past, is dimly lit and hard to follow. Bold, indeed, must be he who would travel that path amid the abysses of his own personality, on the narrow and slippery slope between self-deception and purposeful forgetfulness, down into the region where he is alone with himself, where (as when Faust went down to the Mothers) the impressions of his own life exist only as symbols of their former existence in the real world.

How much patience and self-confidence he will need before he will be justified in saying the sublime words: *Vidi cor meum*! How arduous is the return from this innermost sanctuary to the conflicting world of literary creation, the return from self-contemplation to self-portraiture! If we want an index to the enormous difficulty of such an enterprise, we can find it in the rarity of success. We can count on our fingers the number of those who have achieved it. Even among autobiographies which draw near to perfection, how many gaps there are, how many hazardous leaps, how much padding and patchwork! Always, in art, that which lies nearest to hand is the most difficult; the undertaking one would have thought the most trivial proves the most formidable. Autobiography is the hardest of all forms of literary art.

Why, then, do new aspirants, generation after generation, try to solve this almost insoluble problem? Here an elemental impulse is at work, powerful as an obsession, the inborn longing for self-immortalization. Placed amid an unceasing flux, overshadowed by the perishable, doomed to perpetual transformation, swept away by the irresistible current of time, one molecule among milliards, we are all of us involuntarily spurred on by the intuition of immortality to seek an anchorage in something, no matter what, which shall outlast our ephemeral existence. Begetting and self-portraiture are, in the last analysis, nothing more than two different ways of expressing the same primary function, the same endeavour to cut a notch that will endure for a while in the ever-growing tree of humanity. A self-portrait, therefore, is nothing more than the most intensive form of the will to perpetuate oneself; and early attempts in this direction still lacked the developed artistry of the picture, the elaborated aid of writing. Stone blocks set up over tombs; clay tablets on which, in clumsy, wedge-shaped characters, deeds of heroes were recorded; fragments of bark inscribed with runes—such are the forms in which the earliest self-portraits have come down to us across the void spaces of the millenniums. Long since have the deeds become without meaning, and the language of those mouldering generations has grown incomprehensible. Unmistakably, nevertheless, the records betray the impulse which animated the men and the women who fashioned them, the impulse to portray themselves, to keep themselves in being, by handing down to posterity a trace of the individuality which might thus be preserved when life had fled. The obscure will to self-perpetuation is the elemental urge underlying and initiating every attempt at self-portraiture.

Long, long afterwards, when mankind had become more knowledgeable and more conscious of self, a further connotation was added to the crude and vague impulse towards attesting that one has existed.

Now the individual began to cherish a desire to become aware of himself as an ego, to explain himself to himself for the furtherance of the consciousness of self. When, as St Augustine so well phrases it, a man "becomes a problem to himself", and sets out in search of an answer which will concern him alone among mortals, he unrolls the course of his life before himself like a map, that he may see that course more plainly and understand it better. At this stage, he does not try to explain himself to others, for he wishes, in the first instance, to explain himself to himself. Here he reaches a parting of the ways (we reach it today in every autobiography) between the description of life and the description of experience, portrayal for others and portrayal for the writer's own sake, autobiography that is objectively directed and autobiography that is subjectively directed. Writers belonging to the former group have an impulse towards the public avowal. Confession is their characteristic method, confession before the whole world or confession to the pages of a book. Writers of the latter group are prone to soliloquy, and are usually content with writing diaries. Only persons endowed with an extremely complicated temperament such as Goethe, Stendhal, and Tolstoy, have tried to effect the thoroughgoing synthesis in this field, perpetuating themselves in both forms.

Self-contemplation, however, is nothing more than a preparatory step, and not a momentous one. Thus far, sincerity is easy. The artist's real torment does not come until the work of communication begins; not until then is a heroic candour demanded of the autobiographer. For no less elemental than the urge to be communicative, to let all our brethren know about the uniqueness of our personality, is the counter-urge towards secretiveness, manifesting itself in the form of shame. Just as a woman's innermost being tingles with the longing to surrender her body, while in the conscious she is animated with the desire to keep her body for herself, so the will to confession must wrestle with the spiritual modesty which counsels reserve. Even the vainest among us (above all, the vainest among us) feels that he is not perfect, not so perfect as he would like others to think him. For that reason he would fain keep his less amiable characteristics private, would like the knowledge of his inadequacies and pettinesses to die with him, even while he wishes his likeness to live on among his fellows.

Shame, therefore, is the perpetual adversary of sincerity. With flattering tongue she tries to dissuade us from describing ourselves as we really are, and advises us to depict ourselves as we should like people to see us. The artist may honestly resolve to be

frank, but with feline artifice shame will lead him
astray, will induce him to hide his most intimate self,
to gloss over his defects. Under her promptings, all
unawares, the draughtsman's hand omits or embell-
ishes disfiguring trifles (supremely important, in the
psychological sense), or idealizes characteristic traits
by an adroit distribution of light and shade. One
who is weak enough to follow such promptings will
not achieve self-portraiture; he will not get beyond
self-apotheosis or self-defence. Honest autobiography,
therefore, can never be a care-free narrative. Always
the writer must be on his guard against the whisper-
ings of vanity, must strenuously ward off the tempta-
tions to touch up the picture he is presenting to the
world. For the very reason that nobody else can control the autobiographer's sincerity, that nobody but
himself can hold him to account, he must have a
combination of qualities which will hardly be found
once in a million instances; he must be witness and
judge, accuser and defender, rolled into one.

There is no armour of proof against self-trickery.
However strong a cuirass we make, we can launch a
bullet swift enough to pierce it, and the powers of
self-deception can be intensified to cope with the
powers of self-knowledge. However resolutely a man
may bar the door against falsehood, she will creep in
through a chink. If he study the lore of the mind

that he may learn how to parry her onslaughts, she will discover a new and cleverer thrust which will get in beneath his guard. Like a panther, she will crouch in the shadows, to spring upon him when he is most unprepared. The art of self-deception is refined and sublimated by the wider experience, by the growth in psychological knowledge, designed to avert self-deception. One who manipulates truth roughly will produce lies which are crude and easily recognizable. Not until a man has a subtle mind are his falsehoods subtilized, refined, so that they can be detected only by one as subtle as himself. When thus subtilized, they assume the most perplexing, the most illusive forms; and their most deceptive mask is invariably the semblance of honesty. Just as snakes prefer to lurk among rocks and boulders, so the most dangerous lies are hidden in the shade of seemingly heroic admissions. When you are reading an autobiography, and come to a passage where the narrator appears amazingly frank, attacking himself ruthlessly, it behoves you to walk warily, for the probability is that these reckless avowals, these beatings of a penitent's breast, are intended to conceal some secret which is even more dreadful. One of the arts of confession is to cover up what we wish to keep to ourselves, by boldly disclosing something far more tremendous. Part of the mystery of the sense of shame is that a man will more readily expose his most hideous and repulsive characteristics than bring to light a trifle that might make him appear ridiculous. In every autobiography, that which is above all likely to lead the writer out of the straight path is the dread of arousing the ironical laughter of his readers.

Jean-Jacques Rousseau, with a passion for self-revelation, trumpets his sexual irregularities. In the contrite vein, he deplores that he, author of *Emile*, the famous treatise on education, should have rid himself of his offspring by depositing them in the revolving box at the foundling hospital. Such frankness is suspect. The pseudo-heroic admission was, perhaps, a mask of inhumanity to hide something he found it impossible to acknowledge. The probability is that he never had any children at all, being incompetent to procreate them. Tolstoy, in his *Confession*, shrilly proclaimed himself whoremonger, murderer, thief, and adulterer; but he would not write a line acknowledging the meanness which made him treat his great rival Dostoyevsky so ungenerously. Gottfried Keller, who was familiar with this trick of raising the dust, wrote sarcastically about autobiography in general: "One autobiographer will acknowledge the seven deadly sins, and will conceal the fact that he had only four fingers on his left hand; another will sedulously describe the birthmarks on his back, while

he is as silent as the grave concerning his conscience-
pricks for having borne false witness. When I compare one with another and study their parade of sincerity, I am led to ask myself whether anyone is
sincere, and whether sincerity is possible!"

To expect perfect sincerity in self-portraiture (or
elsewhere) would be as absurd as to expect absolute
justice, freedom, and perfection here on earth. The
most passionate, the most resolute determination to
be true to the facts is frustrated at the outset by the
undeniable fact that we have no trustworthy organ of
truth, that our memory cheats us before we can
begin the work of self-portraiture. Memory is not in
the least like a register kept in a well-ordered office, a
place in which all the documents relating to every
detail of our lives are laid away in store. What we
vaunt as memory is submerged in the rushing stream
of our blood; it is a living organ, subject to the muta-
tions of such organs; it is not a cold-storage chamber,
in which every feeling can retain its natural essence,
its original odour, its primary historical form. In this
complicated flux to which in our haste we give the
specious name of memory, events roll one over the
other like pebbles in the bed of a stream, rubbing
one another down till they become unrecognizable.
They adapt themselves one to another; range themselves this way and that; show a perplexing talent for

mimicry thanks to which they adopt shapes and colours conformable to the groundwork of our desires. Everything, almost without exception, undergoes distortion in this transformatory element. Every subsequent impression overshadows the earlier ones; every new memory modifies the old ones, and may sometimes actually reverse their significance.

Stendhal was the first to recognize this untrustworthiness of memory, and to acknowledge his own incapacity for recording his experiences with historical accuracy. A classical instance is his admission that he could no longer be certain whether the impressions persistent in his mind as to "crossing the Great Saint Bernard" were really vestiges of personal experiences on the famous pass, or memories of an engraving of the region seen by him at a later date. Marcel Proust, Stendhal's spiritual heir, gives an even more striking example of memory's capacity for distortion. In boyhood, he tells us, he saw "Berma" in one of her most famous roles. Before seeing her, his fancy had been full of anticipations, which had been merged in the subsequent real impressions of the actress; at the play, his impressions were influenced by the opinion of his companion, and next day they were further transformed by what he read in the newspapers. When, in after years, he saw Berma in the same part, both he and she having become different persons meanwhile, he was no longer able to decide what had originally been his "true" impression.

Memory, ostensibly an infallible gauge of truth, is in reality an enemy of truth. Before a man can set himself to the description of his life, there must exist in him an organ competent to produce instead of reproducing; he must have a memory capable of exercising poietic functions, competent to select essentials, to emphasize and to slur, to group things organically. Thanks to this creative power of memory, every autobiographer must involuntarily become a romancer when he undertakes to describe his own life. Goethe, wisest among moderns, knew this. When choosing a name for his autobiography, he renounced the claim to tell the truth, the whole truth, and nothing but the truth. *Dichtung und Wahrheit*, poesy and truth, might serve as title for every volume of self-portraiture.

Nevertheless, though it be true that no one can tell the absolute truth about himself, and though everyone who writes his own life must perforce deal with the record imaginatively, the very attempt to be truthful demands supreme integrity in all who write confessions. No doubt the pseudo-confession, as Goethe called it, confession under the rose, in the diaphanous veil of novel or poem, is much easier, and is often far more convincing from the artistic point of view, than an account with no assumption of reserve. Autobiography, precisely because it requires, not truth alone, but naked truth, demands from the artist an act of peculiar heroism; for the autobiographer must play the traitor to himself. Only a ripe artist, one thoroughly acquainted with the workings of the mind, can be successful here. That is why psychological self-portraiture has appeared so late among the arts, belonging exclusively to our own days and to those yet to come. Man had to discover his continents, to fathom his seas, to learn his language, before he could turn his gaze inward to explore the universe of his soul. Classical antiquity had as yet no inkling of these mysterious paths. Caesar and Plutarch, the ancients who describe themselves, are content to deal with facts, with circumstantial happenings, and never dream of showing more than the surface of their hearts.

Before he can throw light into his own soul, a man must be aware of its existence, and this awareness does not begin until after the rise of Christianity. St Augustine's *Confessions* breaks a trail for inward contemplation. Yet the gaze of the famous divine was directed, not so much inward, as towards the congregation he hoped to edify by the example of his own conversion. His treatise was a confession to the community, a model confession; it was purposeful, teleological; it was not an end in itself, comprising its own answer and its own meaning. Many centuries were to pass before Rousseau (that remarkable man who was a pioneer in so many fields) was to draw a self-portrait for its own sake, and was to be amazed and startled at the novelty of his enterprise. "I am planning," he writes, "an undertaking which has no precedent... I wish to present my fellows with the portrait of a man sketched with perfect fidelity to nature, and I am myself this man." With the credulity of every beginner, he still supposes that the ego is "an indivisible unity," and that "truth" is something tangible and palpable. He is still naïve enough to fancy that when the last trump sounds he will appear before the Great Judge and say, pointing to the book in his hand, "This was I." We of a later generation no longer share Rousseau's simple faith. Instead, we have a fuller and hardier knowledge of the multiplicity and profundity of the psyche. In our craving for self-knowledge, we lay bare the nerves and the blood-vessels of every thought and feeling, following them into their finest ramifications. Stendhal, Hebbel, Kierkegaard, Tolstoy, Amiel, the intrepid Hans Jaeger, have disclosed unsuspected realms of self-knowledge by their self-portraiture. Their successors, provided with more delicate implements of research, will be able to penetrate stratum by stratum, room by room, farther and yet farther into our new universe, into the depths of the human mind.

Let this be a consolation to those who have been led to fear that art will decay in a world rendered unduly conscious by the advance of psychological technique. Art does not cease; it merely takes new turns. A decline in mythopoeic faculty was inevitable. Fantasy is ever most vigorous in childhood, and only in the childhood of a nation is it prone to luxuriate in mythology and symbolism. In compensation for the loss of visionary power, we get a capacity for clear and well-substantiated knowledge. Such a trend is obvious in the contemporary novel, which is becoming the embodiment of an exact science of the mind, whereas of old it was content to draw boldly on imagination. Yet in this union of imagination with science, there is no suppression of art; there is merely a renewal of an ancient family tie. When science began, with Hesiod and Heraclitus, it was still poesy, orphic words and soaring hypotheses. Now, after a divorce which has lasted for thousands of years, the investigatory intelligence and the creative have joined hands once more; and poesy, instead of describing a realm of fable, describes the magic of our human life. The unknown wonders of the physical universe can no longer stimulate imagination, now that the world has grown familiar from the tropics to the poles, now that its fauna and its flora are everyday objects of contemplation, even the creatures that dwell in the amethystine abysses of the sea. Everything on the terrestrial globe has been weighed and measured, named and docketed, leaving in the physical realm nothing but the stars as objects for flights of fancy. More and more, therefore, must the spirit, impelled by the undying urge for knowledge, look inward, to probe its own enigmas. The *internum aeternum*, the spiritual universe, still offers art an inexhaustible domain. Man, as his knowledge widens, as he grows more fully conscious, will devote himself ever more boldly to the solution of an insoluble problem, to the discovery of his own soul, to the pursuit of self-knowledge.

Salzburg, Easter, 1928